Match Wits with Super Sleuth Nancy Drew!

Collect the Original
Nancy Drew Mystery Stories®
by Carolyn Keene

Available in Hardcover!

The Secret of the Old Clock
The Hidden Staircase
The Bungalow Mystery
The Mystery at Lilac Inn
The Secret of Shadow Ranch
The Secret of Red Gate Farm
The Clue in the Diary
Nancy's Mysterious Letter
The Sign of the Twisted Candles
Password to Larkspur Lane
The Clue of the Broken Locket
The Message in the Hollow Oak
The Mystery of the Ivory Charm
The Whispering Statue
The Haunted Bridge
The Clue of the Tapping Heels
The Mystery of the Brass-Bound Trunk
The Mystery of the Moss-Covered Mansion
The Quest of the Missing Map
The Clue in the Jewel Box
The Secret in the Old Attic
The Clue in the Crumbling Wall
The Mystery of the Tolling Bell
The Clue in the Old Album
The Ghost of Blackwood Hall
The Clue of the Leaning Chimney
The Secret of the Wooden Lady

The Clue of the Black Keys
Mystery at the Ski Jump
The Clue of the Velvet Mask
The Ringmaster's Secret
The Scarlet Slipper Mystery
The Witch Tree Symbol
The Hidden Window Mystery
The Haunted Showboat
The Secret of the Golden Pavilion
The Clue in the Old Stagecoach
The Mystery of the Fire Dragon
The Clue of the Dancing Puppet
The Moonstone Castle Mystery
The Clue of the Whistling Bagpipes
The Phantom of Pine Hill
The Mystery of the 99 Steps
The Clue in the Crossword Cipher
The Spider Sapphire Mystery
The Invisible Intruder
The Mysterious Mannequin
The Crooked Banister
The Secret of Mirror Bay
The Double Jinx Mystery
Mystery of the Glowing Eye
The Secret of the Forgotten City
The Sky Phantom
Strange Message in the Parchment
Mystery of Crocodile Island
The Thirteenth Pearl

Nancy Drew Back-to-Back
The Secret of the Old Clock/ The Hidden Staircase

Celebrate 60 Years with the World's Best Detective!

The Mystery at Lilac Inn

Suddenly a panel in the wall slid open

The Mystery at Lilac Inn

BY CAROLYN KEENE

GROSSET & DUNLAP
Publishers • New York
A member of The Putnam & Grosset Group

PRINTED ON RECYCLED PAPER

Contents

CHAPTER I

Mysterious Canoe Mishap

"NANCY DREW! How did you and Helen paddle that canoe up here so fast from River Heights?" cried Doris Drake in astonishment.

Nancy, an attractive titian blond, grinned up at her friend. Doris was weeding a flower garden at her home along the riverbank. "How do *you* know when we left home?" Nancy's blue eyes twinkled.

"My friend Phyl told me on the phone just half an hour ago that she'd talked with you, Nancy, at the Elite Drug Store in River Heights."

Nancy looked surprised. "She couldn't have. Helen and I were on our way here at that time."

Slender, pretty Helen Corning, three years older than Nancy, frowned. "You must have a double, Nancy. Better watch out!"

"I can't understand it," Nancy murmured. "You say Phyl *talked* to her and she didn't say it was a mistake?"

1

"That's right, Nancy," said Doris. "But Phyl was wrong, of course. After all, she doesn't know you terribly well. Say, where are you and Helen going?"

"To visit overnight with Emily Willoughby and her aunt at Lilac Inn. They're family friends. Emily and her fiancé—we've never met him— have bought the inn, and Em tells me, plan to run it full time."

Helen added, "Nancy and I are to be Emily's bridesmaids. We'll talk over wedding plans."

"How wonderful!" Doris exclaimed.

Nancy and Helen said good-by and paddled off upstream. The Angus River, a tributary of the Muskoka, was banked on either side with dense shrubbery, willow trees, and wild flowers.

"We're almost to Benton," Nancy said. "The old inn should be just beyond the next bend."

The next second something rammed the canoe violently. The impact capsized the craft, hurling Nancy and Helen into the chilly May water!

Fortunately, the girls were excellent swimmers. Each instinctively grasped her buoyant, water-proof canvas traveling bag, bobbing nearby, and swam to a grassy bank.

"Whew!" said Nancy, as she dropped her bag to the ground. "Are you all right, Helen?"

Her friend nodded, shivering in her bedraggled shirt and slacks, despite the warm sun. "What made us capsize?"

The impact capsized the canoe

Nancy shrugged. She kicked off her moccasins and plunged into the water again to find out, and to retrieve the canoe. It was drifting upside down a short distance away.

After righting the canoe, Nancy towed it to where they had overturned. She ducked her head beneath the unruffled surface, but saw nothing unusual in the twenty-foot-deep water.

"That's strange," she thought. "Maybe we hit a floating log." But this explanation did not fully satisfy her. A drifting log probably would be still in sight, and there was none.

Nancy pushed the canoe toward shore. Helen grabbed the stern, and pulled the canoe far enough up the bank so the girls could examine it. To their relief, it was undamaged.

"Did you see that man with the crew cut in the rowboat?" Helen asked.

"No. Where?"

Helen pointed to a small, high dock fifty feet downstream. She said that while Nancy was swimming, the man had climbed from the water into a rowboat, glanced their way, then gone in the opposite direction.

"He didn't even try to help us!" Helen said indignantly. "Do you think maybe *he* upset our canoe?"

"I don't see how he could have." Nancy smiled. "But he has upset *you*. Let's go!"

The girls stepped back into the canoe and paddled off. As they rounded the next bend, Helen cried, "There's the Lilac Inn dock!"

When the canoe came abreast of the dock, Nancy secured it to a post. The girls hopped out and started up the path that led to the inn. On both sides of the path were groves of lilac trees which displayed a profusion of blooms, from creamy white to deep purple.

As the girls gazed in delight, a voice called, "Nancy! Helen! I'm so glad to see you. But whatever happened?"

"Emily! Pretend I'm hugging you," Nancy said with a laugh, and explained their accident.

Emily Willoughby, a dainty young woman, had chestnut-colored hair, set off to advantage by her white linen dress.

Beside her stood a handsome, well-built man with wavy, black hair. Nancy and Helen assumed the young man was her fiancé, Dick Farnham, but Emily introduced him as John McBride, an old friend of Dick's.

"John is going to be Dick's best man," Emily explained.

John smiled cordially. "Dick and I were boyhood friends in California, and roommates at college. I'm an Army sergeant on a month's leave." He looked at the new arrivals with twinkling eyes. "Emily will tell you why I'm here. And I'm sure glad I am."

"Now don't go making up to my friends, John,"

Emily teased. "Helen is engaged to Jim Archer, who has a position with an oil company overseas, and Nancy—well, she's mighty busy these days."

The visitors laughed, as Emily added, "You girls change into dry clothes at once."

John carried their bags, as Emily led the way along a shrubbed path which opened onto the spacious lawn surrounding Lilac Inn. Helen and Nancy looked with admiration at the historic hotel, erected in Revolutionary times.

"Here are the new guest cottages," Emily said, as they reached a group of twelve trim white units. "And this one is where you'll stay."

She unlocked the door of the second cottage and the friends stepped inside. John set down the bags. "See you girls later," he said.

As Helen admired the attractive colonial-style bedroom, Nancy noticed a look of anxiety in Emily's eyes. But the next instant it vanished.

Nancy and Helen listened with great interest while their friend said that she and Dick were enlarging the inn. "John has been a big help with our projects. Dick is in New York working on publicity for us."

"I'm sure Lilac Inn will be a bang-up success," Nancy told her.

"Oh, I hope so," Emily said. For a fleeting moment Nancy again detected a worried look in the young woman's eyes. Why?

Emily went on, "You're almost the first guests

in our cottage section—John was first. He's staying near you. The official opening of the inn won't be until July first. That is, if we can complete everything by then," she added dubiously.

"If your aunt is here, Em, I'd love to see her," Nancy said.

"Aunt Hazel's been looking forward to seeing you. I'll tell her you've arrived. Come over to the inn after you've unpacked."

Nancy and Helen changed into pastel cotton dresses, put away the few belongings they had brought, then headed for the inn. As they walked across the lawn, they passed gardeners who were pruning trees and cultivating flower beds edged with pansies.

"It's perfectly beautiful here," Helen remarked.

The girls went to the front of the inn, a two-story clapboard building with a one-level wing on either side. All around it were lilac trees and other flowering bushes. Nancy and Helen mounted the wide steps and entered the center hall. Its paneled walls, old staircase, and beautiful cut-glass chandelier made them feel as though they had stepped back into an earlier century.

The reservation desk was in an alcove off the hallway. John McBride was just putting a letter into the outgoing mail slot.

"Hi!" He grinned. "Ready for a tour of inspection? Delighted to escort you."

"We accept." Helen smiled. "After Nancy and I say hello to Emily's Aunt Hazel."

Just then Emily entered the hall. "Aunt Hazel is—er—busy, but she'll be free in a few minutes. In the meantime, I must speak to Mr. Daly, the former owner of Lilac Inn. He's staying to manage the dining room, which we've kept open for business."

She led the girls to a narrow corridor which ran off the lobby. "Why don't you two wait for Aunt Hazel and me in my office? It's the fourth door down."

Nancy and Helen proceeded along the corridor. As they passed the second door, which was partially open, the girls heard a familiar voice say:

"I can't lend you any more money, Maud! Please don't ask me again!"

Before Nancy and Helen could retreat, Aunt Hazel Willoughby walked quickly from the room. She was followed by a younger woman who had an angry look on her rather pretty but petulant face.

"Nancy! Helen!" Emily's aunt exclaimed, stopping short. "How nice to see you both here! I'm so glad you can be Emily's attendants."

"We are too." Nancy smiled and Helen added, "Emily's going to be a lovely bride."

Mrs. Willoughby, a woman of fifty-five, beamed. White hair framed her face in soft waves, and she was impeccably groomed. She introduced her companion as Mrs. Maud Potter, and said she was to be the inn's social director for the summer.

"That sounds exciting," said Nancy pleasantly.

For a moment Maud's eyes narrowed. Then she tossed her head. "I may not be here July first!" she exploded, and walked away rapidly.

The girls, somewhat taken aback, looked inquiringly at Mrs. Willoughby. The older woman, flustered, made no explanation. She excused herself and hurried after Maud.

Nancy and Helen exchanged glances.

"What a way for a social director to act!" Helen said in disgust. "I wonder why the two women were quarreling about money."

At that moment Emily rejoined the girls and led them into her office. The room was cozy, with a braided rug and pine furniture. The desk in front of the window was cluttered with papers.

"Dick's!" Emily laughed. Then she sobered. "He is worried about finances, poor boy! So far he hasn't been able to raise as much capital as we need," she confided. "I had a hard time convincing him to agree to a certain idea of mine."

"Can you tell us about it?" Nancy asked.

Before Emily could answer, there was a cry of pain from somewhere in the garden. The three girls dashed outside through the front entrance.

Apparently one of the gardeners had stumbled into a large hole in a pathway being strewn with gravel. The man was moaning.

"Oh, Hank!" Emily gasped.

The girls hurried to his side and discovered that one of his legs had gone down through some soft earth.

"Pull me out!" the gardener demanded.

With the girls' assistance, Hank was freed.

"I hope your leg's not broken," Emily said solicitously.

Hank shook his head. "Just a bad sprain. I wasn't lookin' where I was goin'. What I can't figure out is how that hole got here. Queer things have been goin' on at this inn. I'm thinkin' of quittin'. Anyhow, I'm goin' home now."

"Oh, don't quit!" Emily cried.

Several other gardeners had rushed up. All denied having dug the hole. Emily asked one of them, a thin, narrow-eyed young man, named Gil Gary, to drive Hank to his house.

The other men returned to their work, but the girls remained at the site of the accident. Emily's face was troubled.

Nancy said impulsively, "Something's bothering you, Em. What is it?"

Emily's whispered reply astonished her friends. "Dick and I seem to have a mysterious enemy. He is trying to jinx Lilac Inn!"

CHAPTER II

Strange Happenings

A JINX on Lilac Inn! Nancy and Helen stared at Emily in astonishment.

"Tell us about it," Nancy urged her friend.

Emily sighed. "I will. I didn't want to worry Aunt Hazel, so I've kept my suspicions to myself."

The chestnut-haired girl said that four days ago her fiancé had left for New York. Prior to that time, everything had been running smoothly at the inn. An hour after Dick's departure, one of the waitresses had come to Emily's office to give notice.

"When I asked her why she was dissatisfied, she said it was because the inn was—was haunted!"

"What did she mean?" Nancy asked.

Emily said she had not taken the statement seriously. "At the time I was sure the waitress, Mary Mason, was just making up an excuse for leaving.

She packed and left on the bus to River Heights that day. Now I'm not so sure she hadn't seen something strange.

"Sunday morning Gil Gary reported that our finest lilac tree near the front entrance had been stolen. No ghost did that!"

"What a shame!" Helen exclaimed.

"Mr. Daly was heartbroken," Emily said unhappily. "Several years ago he rooted this lilac—the Lucie Baltet variety with a lovely pinkish flower. It was just beginning to blossom abundantly.

"The third strange occurrence," Emily continued, "was around twelve o'clock last night. I was awakened by the sound of music and traced it to our record player in the recreation room. No one was there."

"Perhaps someone at the inn was playing a joke," Nancy suggested.

"No. Everyone denied this," Emily answered. "A window in the recreation room was partially open. It looked as though it had been forced. And I know all the windows had been closed earlier."

There was a thoughtful silence for several seconds, then Emily linked arms with her chums. "I won't worry you with any more mysteries," she said. "Let's have lunch and later concentrate on wedding plans."

Near the dining-room door Emily stopped to introduce her friends to a kind-faced, white-haired man. "This is Mr. Daly, the former owner, whom I told you about. I just couldn't get along without him. I'm so glad he decided to stay awhile, even though he wants to retire."

"How do you do?" Nancy and Helen smiled and shook hands, then went to a corner table near an old hutch cabinet.

Nancy's mind was still on the series of events Emily had just related. It *did* sound as if something peculiar was going on at Lilac Inn!

Nancy had learned from her lawyer father, Carson Drew, that a seemingly unrelated chain of events often became a single baffling mystery. The young sleuth had found proof of this in solving several cases herself—her first being *The Secret of the Old Clock,* and more recently, *The Bungalow Mystery.*

Mrs. Willoughby and John McBride joined the girls. Emily asked them where Maud was.

"I believe she's sun-bathing on the dock," Mrs. Willoughby replied. "She ate an early lunch."

There was a tense note in the woman's voice which Nancy quickly detected. The girl detective recalled the conversation she and Helen had overheard that morning. Had further trouble developed?

When Anna, the waitress, brought the first course of beef broth, Emily changed the subject abruptly. "Lilac Inn is really a fascinating place," she said. "The original floors are still intact, and it's rumored that George Washington ate here in the stagecoach days."

John smiled. "According to reports, our first president must have eaten at every dining place in this country!"

During the luncheon of creamed chicken on toast, peas, salad, and iced tea, Helen asked whether Emily had a neighbor who wore his hair in a crew cut. She explained about the man who had rowed off, instead of coming to the girls' rescue, when their canoe capsized. Emily and her aunt shook their heads.

"Not a very gallant guy," John remarked. He asked several questions about the man with the crew cut and seemed very much disappointed when Helen could add nothing more to the description.

Later, Nancy said to John, "Your career in the Army must be interesting. Do you have a special assignment?"

"Wish I could tell you, Nancy. But it's classified, or confidential, to civilians."

"I understand." Nancy smiled. Presently she turned to Emily. "I saw Doris Drake on the way here. Her house isn't far away, is it?"

"About a mile up the road," Emily answered.

After luncheon Emily offered to show Nancy and Helen around the inn and take them on a tour of the extensive grounds.

"I'll get the jeep for that trip," John offered.

Emily showed her friends the parlors and writing room, and the modern wing containing the pine-paneled recreation room.

"Very attractive," Nancy remarked. She spotted a record player in one corner. "Is that the one the intruder used, Emily?"

"Yes. And here's the window which I found forced open last night," Emily pointed out.

Next, Nancy and Helen were escorted upstairs to see Emily's attractive, old-fashioned two-room suite. "When the inn is ready, there'll be accommodations for fifty guests—"

At this instant a piercing shriek came from the garden. The three girls dashed down the stairs and rushed outside.

"The cry came from near the river," said Nancy, running in that direction.

John McBride and two gardeners joined them. They made a thorough search, but found no one.

Emily turned to Nancy with questioning eyes. "Are you thinking what I am—that the person screamed just to frighten us? And make this place almost seem haunted?"

"Yes. But why? Is someone trying to balk your expansion program here?" Nancy suggested.

"Possibly. But I can't figure out the reason," Emily replied. "Well, I'll show you the rest of the house."

She took the visitors to the far wing, where the kitchen was located. Its gleaming wall ovens and natural-stone colonial fireplace, complete with spit, fascinated Nancy.

"Emily, you'll have no trouble filling every room in this inn," she said enthusiastically. "It's absolutely charming!"

"I hope you're right," Emily replied fervently. "If only the mystery haunting this place could be solved! You'll help, Nancy?"

"I'll certainly try, Emily."

The three girls went to the parking lot where John awaited them at the wheel of the jeep. "Hold onto your hats!" he called.

His three hatless passengers grinned as they hopped into the rear seat. The vehicle shot forward and turned into a dirt lane.

Soon they were driving among groves of apple and peach trees. At Emily's request, John stopped the jeep near an apple tree. She got out to examine the leafy branches. "We'll have an abundant crop this season," she commented. "There are lots of tiny apples forming."

John had climbed out also. Suddenly he stooped and examined the ground.

"What are you looking at?" Nancy called to him.

"A big fat beetle." John laughed.

Nancy chuckled, but she had the feeling that John had been evasive in his reply. As the jeep started off, she looked back. There was a trail of marks leading toward the river.

"They look like flipper tracks," she thought. "I wonder if John made them or if he suspects someone else did."

Later, when the young people returned to the inn, they found Maud Potter on the patio. Nancy was amazed at the change in the woman's manner. Now she was smiling broadly as she waved a folded newspaper.

"Nancy!" she cried effusively. "You're a skin-diving celebrity!"

"What do you mean?" Nancy asked, puzzled, as Mrs. Willoughby joined the group.

Maud opened the paper and pointed to page one of the River Heights *Evening News.*

"Why, Nancy Drew!" Helen exclaimed. "Your picture—and a write-up! You never breathed a word!"

Everyone clustered around to see the picture of Nancy in a bathing suit, diver's mask, and flippers and the accompanying article. The caption read:

Daughter of Local Lawyer, Carson Drew, Learns Her A-B Seas in Skin Diving.

The article went on to tell that Nancy had just completed a course in advanced skin diving in the Muskoka River, and that she had finished first in total points in the twenty-student group.

" 'When asked by our reporter where she hoped to practice the sport,' " John read aloud, " 'Miss Drew replied she would like to skin-dive in both salt and fresh water. This writer strongly suspects that there will be times when she will use her newly acquired knowledge in solving mysteries at which Miss Drew, we understand, is proficient.' "

With an admiring glance, John said, "Meet a fellow frogman. I practically grew up in flippers."

"Really? Oh, I have a wonderful idea!"

Nancy said she would still like to find out, if possible, what had upset her canoe so suddenly. "Maybe there *is* some submerged object I didn't notice. It could be a hazard to other people in boats. John, why don't you take a look underwater at that same spot?"

"How about both of us going?" John suggested, smiling.

Emily spoke up. "Nancy, you and Helen must stay here longer. You can work on the mystery and also go skin diving with John."

Both girls accepted eagerly. "We'll paddle home tomorrow," said Nancy, "pick up more clothes and my diving equipment, then come back."

For the rest of the afternoon, the three girls discussed the subject of gowns to be worn by Emily's bridal attendants. Nancy and Helen were delighted to learn that the color was to be lilac pink.

"By the way, Em," Helen said, "do you know where lilacs came from originally?"

Their hostess nodded. "A German traveler brought the flower from the Orient to Europe in the sixteenth century. Eventually the lilac was introduced to America."

All this time Nancy had noted that Emily was doing her best to seem cheerful, and Maud too continued to act carefree. Emily had arranged a steak cook-out on the patio, and the social director joined in the lively banter. When they finished eating, she brought out a guitar.

"How about some Western tunes?" she suggested gaily.

"Fine. Let's all sing," Helen answered.

At eleven o'clock the group said good night and the River Heights girls tumbled into bed.

The next morning Nancy had just finished dressing when there was a knock on the cottage door. John called out:

"Phone call for you, Nancy, at the desk in the lobby. The cottage phones aren't connected yet."

"Thank you." Nancy hurried to the lobby and picked up the receiver. "Hello? . . . Why, Hannah! What's the trouble?"

Hannah Gruen was the Drews' housekeeper, and had "mothered" Nancy since the age of three when her own mother had passed away.

"Oh, Nancy!" Hannah sounded almost hysterical. "Come home right away! Your father isn't here, and someone broke into the house last night!"

CHAPTER III

A Stolen Charge Plate

NANCY was shocked by Hannah's news. "Have you called the police about the prowler?" she asked the housekeeper.

"No. I wanted to tell you first. I didn't know what had happened until I carried some clean clothes to your room. The second floor seems to be the only place disturbed."

Hannah explained that she had tried to reach Mr. Drew at his hotel in Cleveland, where he was working on a case. But the lawyer had been out.

"I'll be home as soon as possible," Nancy promised. "In the meantime, please notify Chief McGinnis."

"I will, Nancy. Good-by."

Nancy was just about to put down the phone, when she heard a click on the line. Instantly she wondered if someone at Lilac Inn had been purposely listening in on her call.

Before Nancy could speculate further, Emily joined her. Quickly Nancy gave her friend Hannah's report. "I must borrow a car and go right home," she said.

Emily expressed concern about the apparent burglary. "I hope nothing valuable was taken. But, Nancy, you must have breakfast before you go." Emily led the way to the dining room.

Nancy asked her where the other telephones at the inn were located and mentioned the fact that someone might have been eavesdropping on her conversation.

"Every room has an extension," Emily said. "But the only ones connected right now, besides the desk phone, are in the kitchen, my bedroom, my aunt's, and the recreation room."

The young sleuth hastily excused herself. "I'd like to make a few inquiries, Em. Meet me at the table, will you?"

Nancy went into the kitchen. She saw Anna, the waitress, and asked the girl if anyone had used the telephone within the past few minutes. No one had. Then Nancy hurried to the recreation room. It was empty.

When Nancy reached the dining room, she found Emily at the table alone. "Did you learn anything?" Emily asked.

"No."

Emily whispered, "I just remembered, Nancy. Maud had her phone hooked up yesterday."

At that moment Maud came into the dining room. Nancy learned that Maud had just returned from a walk along the river. A few minutes later Mrs. Willoughby, Helen, and John arrived. None had used the phone that morning.

"Guess that click didn't mean an eavesdropper at the inn," Nancy thought.

The others were sympathetic upon hearing her reason for returning home immediately. John promptly offered to drive Nancy in the jeep. But Mrs. Willoughby laughed and said, "I can give you a more comfortable ride, Nancy."

As she started to explain, Anna came to take the orders of those at the table.

"I have to drive to the River Heights Bank this morning," Mrs. Willoughby went on, "to get Emily's diamonds from the safe-deposit box. I'd be delighted to have company."

Before Nancy could reply, Maud Potter repeated shrilly, "Emily's *diamonds?*"

Mrs. Willoughby nodded. "As you know, I've been Emily's guardian for five years, since her parents were killed in the plane crash. Her mother's will states that she's to receive the jewels when she's twenty-one."

Emily dimpled. "That's in two weeks. But I coaxed Aunt Hazel into letting me have them earlier. I'm going to sell enough to help Dick and me with expenses at the inn."

Nancy smiled. "That must be the plan you told me about yesterday."

"That's right." Emily's eyes sparkled.

Maud had been listening intently. She said to Mrs. Willoughby, "You told me there were twenty unset diamonds. I suppose they are worth quite a bit?"

Mrs. Willoughby smiled. "Yes. Over fifty thousand dollars."

Maud remarked pointedly, "You'd better be careful, Hazel. Some people would love to get their hands on those jewels."

As soon as Mrs. Willoughby finished her toast and coffee, she arose from the table. "Nancy," she said, "I'll get the car."

The three girls excused themselves and went outside. "Perhaps, Helen," Nancy said, "you'd like to stay at the inn. I'll be driving back, and can stop at your house to pick up whatever clothes you need."

"Thanks, Nancy. I'd like to stay. I'll phone Mother."

Emily asked if Nancy would have a chance to do her a favor in River Heights. "I'd ask Aunt Hazel, but she wants to get back here as soon as possible with my diamonds."

"I'll be glad to. What is it, Em?"

"Find out if the Empire Employment Agency has any waitresses available."

"Did you get Mary Mason through them?" Nancy asked.

"No. She stopped here. But her references were excellent, so I engaged her."

"I'll be happy to do the errand for you, Emily," Nancy said.

Mrs. Willoughby pulled up in her black sedan and Nancy climbed in front. John had come outside too.

"Don't forget," he said to her, "we have a skindiving date when you get back."

At that moment Maud Potter hurried from the inn to the car. "I'll come along, if you don't mind," the social director said blithely.

She hopped in beside Nancy without waiting for an invitation. Mrs. Willoughby's lips tightened, but she made no comment. Good-bys were exchanged and the car started off.

Soon the sedan was speeding along the main highway. "Any ideas about your burglar?" Maud asked Nancy.

"No," Nancy admitted. "Except he might have been trying to break into Dad's safe."

Maud cocked her head. "Does your father keep important papers at home?"

"Sometimes," Nancy replied noncommittally. She tried to hide her annoyance at the woman's inquisitiveness.

Mrs. Willoughby frowned disapprovingly. "Don't ask so many questions, Maud."

The social director shrugged. Once more she turned to Nancy. Arching her eyebrows coyly, she said, "I'd love to meet your dad sometime. I understand he is a widower."

"This is the last straw!" Nancy thought. Though annoyed, she had to suppress a smile at the woman's remark. Maud Potter certainly was not the type of person to interest her father!

"Dad keeps very busy, and travels a lot on his cases," Nancy said coolly. "He's away now."

Maud's coyness vanished. "I see. No time for social life," she said sarcastically.

To Nancy's relief, the woman spoke hardly at all for the balance of the trip. Presently Mrs. Willoughby pulled up into the winding driveway of the Drews' handsome brick home, surrounded by a velvety green lawn.

Nancy expressed her thanks for the ride and said good-by. She hurried into the house, for the moment forgetting Lilac Inn completely. Hannah Gruen greeted her with, "Oh, Nancy dear. I'm so glad you're back. I've been frantic!"

Nancy hugged the pleasant-faced woman, who said that Police Chief McGinnis had stopped at the house to investigate the burglary.

"No silver or other valuables are missing," Hannah went on. "But your room is a mess. Whoever was here must have been after something you keep there." The woman frowned worriedly.

Nancy dashed up the stairs. What a sight met

her eyes as she entered her room! Bureau and chest drawers were open, their contents spilling out. Perfume bottles lay overturned on her dressing table. Clothes had been pulled from the closet and flung onto the bed and floor.

Mrs. Gruen, who had followed Nancy, explained, "Chief McGinnis wanted me to leave everything like this for you to see."

Nancy nodded. "How was the house entered?"

"Through the back door," Hannah replied. "The chief said the intruder must be an expert lock picker and burglar. He left no fingerprints."

Nancy hurried into her father's bedroom. Nothing here had been disturbed apparently. She went into the adjoining den and was relieved to see that the thief had not broken into the safe.

"The only thing missing from here is my picture," Nancy reported to Hannah.

"Oh, dear! What does it all mean?" the housekeeper asked worriedly.

Before Nancy could continue, the phone rang, and she answered it.

"Miss Nancy Drew?" a woman asked.

"Yes."

"This is Burk's Department Store. I'm Mrs. Reilly of the fine jewelry department. I made a terrible mistake when I sold you that watch this morning. The price was one hundred and twenty-five dollars, not fifty as I told you. Do you still want to keep it?"

Utterly astounded, Nancy said, "Mrs. Reilly, I didn't buy a watch this morning! I was out of town."

"Isn't your charge account number 10–4875?"

"Wait, please. I'll check."

Nancy hurried to open the desk drawer where she had put Burk's charge plate. Its leather case was there, but the metal plate was not inside. "It has been stolen!" Nancy exclaimed.

With a sense of foreboding, she returned to the phone. "I'll drive right down to see the manager," Nancy said. "My charge plate has been stolen, I'm afraid."

Nancy paused long enough to tell Hannah of her discovery, and to notify Chief McGinnis. The officer said he would meet her at the store manager's office.

Just as she was about to enter Burk's, Nancy stopped short. To her amazement, she saw Maud Potter entering the Empire Employment Agency office across the street.

"Now what's up?" Nancy wondered. "Is Maud trying to engage a waitress for the inn, too?"

Puzzled, she hurried into the department store and took an elevator to the third-floor office of the manager, Mr. Goldsmith.

"I'm Nancy Drew," she greeted him pleasantly. "I want to explain—"

She got no further. With a stern look, the manager said curtly, "I know all about the watch you claim not to have bought early this morning. But how about those other items you carried away?"

Dumfounded, Nancy could only echo, *"Other items?"*

Grimly the manager continued, "I don't know what your game is, Miss Drew. But unless you have a twin, you owe Burk's Department Store for merchandise worth two thousand dollars!"

CHAPTER IV

Address Unknown

NANCY felt she must be dreaming. Not only had
the thief charged two thousand dollars to her account, but the store manager seemed to believe
that Nancy herself had made the purchases.

"I must have a double!" she thought. "Doris
Drake's friend Phyl was right in thinking she was
talking to me. Someone is impersonating me! It's
possible this person or a friend of hers broke into
our house, took the charge plate, and some of my
clothes for her to wear!"

Outwardly, Nancy tried to appear calm. "I
couldn't have bought those things, Mr. Goldsmith," she insisted. "This is the first time today
I've been in Burk's."

For answer, the manager pressed a buzzer.
Three women entered. He introduced them as
Mrs. Reilly, Miss Coogan, and Mrs. Watson.

"Mrs. Reilly sold you the watch," said Mr.

Goldsmith. "From Miss Coogan you bought an expensive mink stole. Next, you purchased two high-priced dresses in Mrs. Watson's department. Ladies, do you identify this girl?"

The saleswomen nodded. Each one identified her as Nancy Drew, the young woman she had waited on, and who had signed sales slips for each purchase.

"This is preposterous!" Nancy cried, her blue eyes flashing. "Someone is impersonating me. She stole my charge plate. I want to see those sales slips."

Just then, to Nancy's relief, Chief McGinnis entered the office. He and the Drews were old friends, and he greeted Nancy cordially.

Mr. Goldsmith spoke up. "Glad you're here, Chief. I was just going to call you." He explained what had happened.

The police officer replied calmly, "If Nancy Drew says she didn't buy anything, she didn't. Let's get down to facts, Mr. Goldsmith. I'm here to help Miss Drew, and Burk's also."

The chief quizzed the salesclerks briefly. After hearing their stories, he said gravely, "Nancy, I'm afraid this young woman who resembles you so closely—and forged your signature on the sales slips—may continue to take advantage of it."

Nancy smiled ruefully. "I realize that." She was more convinced of this than ever when the sales slips were brought to the office. The forgery was excellent. Nancy's impersonator must have carefully practiced the signature on the charge plate.

Mr. Goldsmith sighed wearily. "I'm sorry, Miss Drew, about this whole matter, and that I suspected you of dishonesty."

"That's all right," she replied. "The main thing is to track down the culprit and get back your stolen property."

She asked the clerks what her "twin" had been wearing. "It was a lovely light-blue dress," replied Mrs. Reilly. "Printed silk, with white flowers."

Nancy gasped. "I have a dress like that. And I don't remember seeing it in my closet today."

"The woman no doubt took it," the police chief said, frowning. "Nancy, be very careful. This impersonation may mean not only annoyance, but possible danger for you."

Mr. Goldsmith promised that Burk's private detective and all the store's sales personnel would be on the lookout for Nancy's unknown double.

As the young sleuth left the store with Chief McGinnis, she said to him, "I wonder if this person actually is my double or is only cleverly made up to resemble me."

The officer frowned. "If it's the latter, the thief will be harder to catch. She may not pose as Nancy Drew again for some time. But I'll have my men start working on the case from every possible angle." He admitted that no clues to the thief at the Drew home had been found. "I'll post a twenty-four-hour guard at your home."

"Good," Nancy said. "Hannah will feel much better, since I have to return to Lilac Inn this afternoon, and Dad's away."

Nancy said good-by to the chief and hurried across the street to the employment agency. She wondered if by chance Maud Potter might still be there. But when Nancy entered the office, the only person there was the woman manager, seated at a desk.

"Can I help you?" she asked Nancy.

"I'm here at the request of the new owners of Lilac Inn," Nancy replied. "Has anyone else been in to ask about a waitress to work out there?"

"No."

As Nancy asked her next question, she was thinking, "Why was Maud in here?" Aloud she said, "Have you any waitresses on your list?"

"Not at present. We'll call you if any apply."

On impulse, Nancy asked her, "Could you tell me if you've ever had a Miss Mary Mason on your waitress list?"

The woman opened a nearby file and flipped through a folder. "No, we haven't."

Nancy thanked the manager and left the agency. When she arrived home and told Hannah the latest developments, the housekeeper was more upset than ever.

"I feel in my bones that this impersonator is up to something sinister," she declared. "I wish your dad were home."

"You'll be safe here, Hannah," Nancy said assuringly, and told Mrs. Gruen that a policeman would be assigned to guard the house. "And speaking of Dad, I'm going to call him right now and ask him if he took that picture of me with him."

"While you do that, I'll fix some lunch for us," Mrs. Gruen offered. "You must be starved. It's two o'clock."

Nancy went to the hall telephone and a minute later was requesting the switchboard operator at the Cleveland hotel to ring Mr. Drew's room.

"Hello?" came the lawyer's deep, resonant voice.

"Hi, Dad! How good to hear you!" Nancy said happily.

She gave him an account of the burglary and succeeding events. Carson Drew was greatly concerned. "Nancy," he added in a troubled voice, "I didn't bring your photograph with me. Your double must have taken it. She has already fooled four persons who don't know you well. With the help of the picture, she may try something bolder," he stated.

"You think this girl has some ulterior motive other than faking my charge account, don't you, Dad?"

"I'm afraid so. Be on your guard, Nancy. Try

to stay with a group as much as possible, particularly after you return to Lilac Inn."

The lawyer added that he would be home the next day. "I'll look into the whole affair then."

Nancy promised to be careful and said good-by. She and Hannah sat down and ate lunch. Finally Nancy said she had to pack and leave.

"But first I'm going to try locating that waitress Mary Mason." Nancy picked up the telephone directory and thumbed through it until she reached the *M*'s. She called two families named Mason, but each denied having a relative Mary.

"Probably," Nancy surmised, "Mary did not live in this area."

Deep in thought she went upstairs and took a suitcase from her closet. Nancy quickly placed additional garments in it, then gathered up her skin-diving equipment: green rubber fins, a diving mask, and an aqualung. Finally, Nancy packed a rubber suit which would insulate her body against the cold river water, and an underwater camera her father had given her.

Nancy kissed Hannah good-by and got into her convertible. She drove to the Cornings' home and picked up Helen's suitcase, then set out for Lilac Inn.

Her thoughts revolved around the mystery out there and also on the problem of her impersonator. "No one could look enough like me to be absolutely identical. Why, even identical twins have distinguishing characteristics," she told herself with a smile, "such as the shape of fingernails, voice tones, and facial expressions."

The late-afternoon traffic on the highway to Benton was becoming heavy. Nancy turned from the main road onto a very narrow, less-used one. Presently, in her mirror, she saw a red panel truck behind her coming along at an alarming speed. Nancy, at the same time, noted an arrow indicating a sharp curve ahead. She braked and motioned the truck driver to slow down.

Either he did not see her signal, or was ignoring it. Instead of slowing down, the truck's speed increased, as if to pass her. The curve was not wide enough for two cars to go side by side. On Nancy's right was a deep ditch, filled with water.

She had no choice but to start around the curve. To her horror, the other vehicle was already edging around her left fender. Nancy glimpsed a chrome eagle ornament on the truck's hood.

A split second later her convertible was forced over into the ditch!

CHAPTER V

Blackout!

As NANCY's convertible leaned precariously, its right wheels in the ditch, the panel truck roared on around the bend and out of sight. Nancy braked her car to a stop, thankful it had not turned over.

"That driver ought to have his license revoked!" she thought indignantly. She knew it would be difficult to get out of the muddy ditch. "Well, I'll have a try," she decided. "Here goes!"

She tried to rock the car gently back and forth to gain momentum. The right tires spun crazily and sank lower into the mire.

Nancy tried again. No use. She feared it might be some time before a car would come along in this deserted area. Finally she decided to search for some objects to force under the right wheels for traction.

Just then, Nancy heard an automobile ap-

proaching. "Thank goodness!" she murmured a
moment later. "A State Police car."

It drew up and parked at the side of the road.
A young officer hopped out.

"Having trouble, miss?" he asked. "Lieutenant
Brice, Benton State Police Barracks," he said
pleasantly.

Nancy introduced herself, then explained. He
asked if she had noted the truck's license plates.
"No," she replied, but described the truck and
the chrome eagle ornament on its hood.

Lieutenant Brice said that if he found the
truck, he would see that the driver was brought
to court.

"I have a tow chain in my car. I'll try to pull
you out. Keep the engine in gear."

Five minutes later the convertible was out of
the ditch. Nancy thanked the trooper for his
help, then drove off.

It was almost six o'clock when Nancy pulled
into the Lilac Inn parking lot. She went at once
to the patio, where the Willoughbys, Maud,
Helen, and John were gathered.

"I'm glad you could return in time for supper,
Nancy," said Mrs. Willoughby.

The others plied the girl detective with questions about the Drews' burglar. Nancy gave an account of her day's experiences, concluding with
the reckless truck driver.

"Why, how terrible!" Emily exclaimed.

"The nerve of someone impersonating you!" Helen bristled.

Nancy smiled wryly. "I'd certainly like to know what the girl's purpose is."

Abruptly, Maud changed the subject. To Emily she said, "I dropped into the Empire Employment Agency this morning. A waitress walked in to apply, so I told her to report here tomorrow for an interview. Her name is Jean Holmes."

"But I asked—" Emily broke off when Nancy gave her a warning look.

Maud evidently did not notice this, and added sweetly, "I knew another waitress was needed here. I just wanted to make myself useful."

"I see. Thank you," Emily said coolly.

Later, after Maud had excused herself to dress for supper, Emily burst out, "Maud makes me so angry! Why doesn't she tend to her own job!"

"Don't pick on her, dear!" Mrs. Willoughby retorted. "She's had a hard enough time lately." Rising, Emily's aunt said she wanted to confer with Mr. Daly and went off.

The four young people were left alone. Nancy asked Emily how Maud had been chosen as social director for Lilac Inn.

"Aunt Hazel asked us to," Emily replied. In a whisper she added, "I wish Maud would concentrate more on our recreational program. Nancy, why did you give me the high-sign?"

Nancy told of having seen Maud enter the

agency, and of being informed by the manager later that no one had inquired about a waitress.

Emily sighed. "I'll be so glad when Dick gets back. Especially if any more strange things happen around here."

"Emily, you've nothing to worry about," John declared. "Everything will be fine."

The young man stood up, saying he had a supper engagement in town. "Sorry I'll miss the festivities, Emily. I'll see your glittering gems later."

Emily, her face brightening, explained to Nancy that her aunt had planned a festive meal that evening. "To celebrate my receiving the diamonds."

"That'll be fun," Nancy said. "Helen, let's go now and change our clothes."

The two girls took the suitcases from Nancy's convertible. As they unpacked in the cottage and dressed, Helen discussed Nancy's impersonator.

"It's positively creepy, Nancy," she said worriedly. "Your double doesn't sound like an ordinary thief."

The girls quickly finished dressing. Nancy had put on a pink sheath dress and pumps. Helen wore an aqua organdy. They went to the patio where Emily joined them a minute later. She said that Jean Holmes, the waitress, had arrived unexpectedly for her interview. The girl had explained that she had heard of a second position, and wanted to make a decision immediately.

"Jean seems quite satisfactory," Emily stated. "She'll move in here tomorrow and start work."

Maud Potter joined the girls. "I'm so glad you approve my choice, Emily," she said ingratiatingly. "Now, let's have supper and see your diamonds."

Emily led the group to a small private dining room which opened off the larger room and overlooked a garden. They said good evening to Mr. Daly who stood just outside the connecting door.

Mrs. Willoughby was waiting for them near an open window and greeted Emily with a "Happy Birthday in advance, dear!"

"Oh, thank you, Aunt Hazel. Everything looks divine!"

All the girls admired the table, set with gleaming silver, a creamy lace cloth, and a beautiful birthday cake surrounded by red roses for a centerpiece. Soft light from colonial wall fixtures completed the picture, as shadows danced on the old paneled walls.

Emily's aunt beamed. "I want everything to be perfect tonight," she said.

Mrs. Willoughby sat at one end of the table, her back to the open windows, Emily opposite her. By the time the main course was finished, it was almost dark outside. Then the candles were lighted on the cake and everyone joined in singing "Happy Birthday" as Emily blew out the candles.

After dessert, Mrs. Willoughby asked Mr. Daly

Nancy realized what the sale of the diamonds would mean to Lilac Inn

to close the door to the private dining room. The elderly man nodded understandingly and shut the door.

Mrs. Willoughby withdrew a white velvet jewel case from her handbag. Getting up, she went to place it on the table before Emily, then returned to her chair. With a smile she said:

"This is a wonderful moment for you, Emily dear—the inheritance from your mother. I only hope these gems will bring you happiness."

Nancy noticed that Emily's hands trembled slightly as she opened the case. Everyone gasped. Against the white satin lining were the twenty diamonds which glowed and flashed.

"Oh!" Emily exclaimed. "Aren't they beautiful!" She set the box on the table.

Maud stared in fascination, and Nancy and Helen expressed their delight at Emily's good fortune. Nancy realized what the sale of these gems would mean in financial assistance to Lilac Inn.

Emily arose and gave her aunt a hug and kiss. "Oh, Aunt Hazel, you're a love. I'm sure Mother would understand my wanting to use the gems for my future and Dick's."

Suddenly the group was startled by a clattering crash from the adjoining dining room. Simultaneously, the lights went out. Nancy hurriedly rose and flicked the wall switch back and forth, but the room remained dark.

"Mr. Daly," called Emily, opening the door,

"will you please check the fuse box in the cellar?"

"I will," he replied. "I think a main circuit's blown—all our lights are out."

"Oh, dear," fretted Mrs. Willoughby. "What a trying bother!"

"Yes. These old buildings are so undependable," Maud said crossly. "Something's always breaking down."

"This can happen in a modern one, too," Nancy said in defense of Lilac Inn. Maud merely sniffed in annoyance.

To everyone's relief, John was heard shouting from the garden, "Hold everything! I'll be right in!"

But as John stepped through the open window, the lights came on again. The next instant Emily, returning to her chair, gave a horrified cry.

"My diamonds! They're gone!"

The others gasped in disbelief. Hazel Willoughby, ash-white, stared at the place on the table where the velvet case had rested. Then she pitched forward in a faint.

"Oh!" Emily sobbed fearfully.

"Your aunt will be all right," said Nancy, who had jumped up. Quickly she and Helen dampened napkins with ice water from the tumblers and applied these to the woman's head and wrists. In a few seconds Mrs. Willoughby revived.

"I'm sorry," she apologized weakly. "Such an

awful shock—the diamonds vanishing into thin air."

Emily insisted that her aunt go to her room and lie down.

"I'll be all right, dear. Really. What do we do now?" Mrs. Willoughby looked around helplessly.

"We'd better keep this to ourselves," John said. "Otherwise, dinner guests will be upset. I'll check outside for prowlers. However, the thief didn't go out this window."

Nancy decided to do some sleuthing for the thief in the building and hurried into the main dining room. The only guests were two elderly women, waiting to pay their bill. Nancy learned from them that the waitress Anna had accidentally dropped a tray, which caused the clattering noise just before the lights went out. The ladies were sure that no one else but Mr. Daly had been in the room at the time.

Nancy next went into the kitchen, where the cooks and waitresses were cleaning up after the evening meal. The girl detective asked where each of them had been when the inn was plunged into darkness. All the women except Anna replied that they had been in the kitchen.

Anna gave Nancy a curious look. "Why do you ask?"

The young detective explained that Emily Willoughby wanted to be sure no one had been hurt by an unexpected fall during the blackout.

Nancy left the kitchen and hurriedly went through the other first-floor rooms, but saw no one. As she walked back toward the private dining room, Nancy met Mr. Daly in the lobby. He told her that he had found nothing wrong with the lighting system.

"I can't understand what happened," he said, then added, "I just heard from Emily about the missing jewels. How dreadful!"

John came in at that moment and said he had found no prowler on the grounds. "By this time the jewel thief is undoubtedly far away," he concluded.

As Nancy returned with him to the private dining room, she was deep in thought. Logically, the only ones who could have taken the diamonds were she and her four dining companions! "But that's absolutely unlikely," Nancy told herself. She reported her findings to the others.

Maud Potter's eyes narrowed. "I suppose you think Emily should search us!" she said nastily to Nancy.

"Maud!" Emily protested. "Nancy meant no such thing."

Maud paid no attention, but turned on Mrs. Willoughby, who was still pale. "You can blame yourself, Hazel—announcing in a public dining room this morning that you were going to get Emily's diamonds!"

"I know." Mrs. Willoughby sighed. But Emily put a comforting arm around her, and gave Maud a look of disapproval.

"Let's all search this room," Nancy proposed quickly. "We might find some clue."

Everyone but Maud readily agreed. She sat sullen-faced, while the others looked carefully in corners and under tables and chairs.

Nancy herself was scrutinizing the area where Emily had sat. Suddenly her keen eyes spotted three tiny pale-purple lilac buds on the floor. One —two—three—she counted, then saw a fourth bud lying near the wall to the right of Emily's chair. Aside from the centerpiece, there were no other flowers in the room.

"How did lilac buds get in here?" Nancy mused. There was no sign of footprints near them.

Saying nothing, Nancy picked one up. It was fresh. She looked at the wall thoughtfully and closely.

Everyone watched in amazement as the titian-blond girl began to tap the wall, then listen intently.

Nancy motioned them not to say a word. She continued tapping, until she tried one spot which sounded different. It had a hollow ring. Nancy pressed against the wooden wall. Suddenly a panel slid aside noiselessly.

CHAPTER VI

Uncanny Recoveries

JOHN and the others gaped in astonishment as the panel in the wall slid open. "Nancy, you're terrific!" John exclaimed, handing her his flashlight.

Everyone crowded behind Nancy, as she beamed the light into a wood-walled closet. It had a musty odor.

"I don't remember seeing this in the floor plans of the inn," Emily said, puzzled, as Nancy stooped and shone the flash on something on the floor. It was a crushed, but still fresh lilac flower!

"It was those other blossoms which made me think there might be a concealed entrance into this room."

"Nancy, you're a genius," said Mrs. Willoughby. "I never dreamed this spot was here. The thief must have been hiding in the closet."

"But where did he go?" John asked.

Nancy was feeling the rear wall of the closet. Her fingers touched a small metal latch. She turned it. A second panel slid open soundlessly. Beyond was the coat closet off the lobby of the inn!

"This must be how the jewel thief got in and out of this dining room," Nancy announced. She walked on into the lobby, followed by the others.

"Look!" Helen exclaimed, and pointed to a lilac bud near the front door.

Nancy examined the bud which proved to be fresh and moist. "The thief probably wore a sprig of lilacs. That makes me think the person was a woman."

Mr. Daly agreed with Nancy. He admitted that he had not known of the hidden closet, and was perplexed as to who could have learned of it.

"These panel openings must have fallen into disuse before I purchased the inn," he remarked.

"One thing's certain," said Nancy. "The thief not only has an intimate knowledge of the original floor plan of Lilac Inn but also knew two other things: that Emily was to receive her diamonds tonight, and where Mrs. Willoughby was to present them."

"Too bad I didn't get back sooner tonight," said John, frowning. "I might have met the thief. Incidentally, she must have had an accomplice to work the lighting system."

"But how could they communicate at just the

right moment if one of them was in the cellar?" Helen asked.

"I can answer that," said Mr. Daly. "The panel board for the light control is directly under that private dining room. The floor is worn so thin that conversation upstairs can be heard down there."

Nancy nodded. "After the person in the cellar was sure the thief was hidden again, he or she turned on the lights to make the whole thing look like a temporary outside power failure."

"What shall we do now?" Maud asked nervously.

"Call the police immediately," Nancy advised.

"No!" Emily cried out.

Everyone looked at her in surprise. Emily flushed, but remained adamant.

"If people hear we've had a robbery," she argued, "it may discourage them from coming to Lilac Inn. Calling in the police will mean newspaper publicity. Dick and I have worked too hard to risk it."

"It will be a shame if you don't recover the diamonds," Helen spoke up. "But if you report the theft, at least you can collect the insurance, Emily, and use that money for the inn as you planned."

At this remark Mrs. Willoughby's face again turned ash-white and the others thought she was about to faint again. "Insurance. Insurance," she said hoarsely. "There isn't any! I thought the jewels were safe in the bank vault and let the insurance policy lapse!"

Everyone listening was stunned and tears came to Emily's eyes. She turned to Nancy and asked in a trembling voice, "What shall I do?"

It was Helen who spoke up. "Have Nancy take over the case of your missing diamonds, Emily. I guarantee she'll unearth them!"

All the others backed Helen's suggestion eagerly except Maud. The social director merely raised her eyebrows.

The amateur sleuth smiled. "I'll be glad to do what I can, Emily, but this is a big assignment. If I don't succeed very soon, will you promise to notify the police?"

"It's a bargain, Nancy."

John whistled. "Miss Nancy Drew, detective, you're not going to have much time for skin diving."

Nancy laughed. "I'll find time."

John cautioned the Willoughbys to make sure all first-floor doors and windows were kept locked at night. He himself went outside to make another tour of the grounds. Emily reassured her unhappy aunt and persuaded her to go to bed. Maud said she would follow.

The three girls decided to check the window and door locks in the various rooms. Emily took the kitchen and offices, while Nancy and Helen headed for the other rooms. Minutes later they met in the lobby to report everything locked.

Helen gave a huge sigh. "Nancy, aren't you exhausted after all this excitement?"

Nancy admitted that she was a bit tired. "Two burglaries in one day and a car mishap are quite enough." She smiled wearily. "Helen, what's your theory about the theft of Emily's diamonds?"

The dark-haired girl hesitated. "I'm sure it's an outside job but—"

"Out with it, Miss Corning," Nancy urged. "Whom do you suspect?"

"John McBride!" her friend blurted. "I like him very much, but he was away most of today. Yet Emily said he was here to help fix up the inn during Dick's absence."

"Yes, she did," Nancy admitted. "But I can't believe John has anything to do with either the theft or the mysterious happenings at Lilac Inn."

The young sleuth's eyes had been roving back and forth across the floor, since it was instinctive with her to be hunting for clues whenever a mystery confronted her. Something glinted in a corner under a chair. She went to pick it up as Emily came into the lobby.

"What is it?" Emily asked.

"Believe it or not, it's my stolen charge plate!" Nancy answered. "I may be jumping to conclusions, but I'm sure now that my impersonator is the jewel thief. She dropped the charge plate from her pocket or purse, probably when she put the jewel case in it."

"This is positively eerie," Helen remarked. "Maybe that fake Nancy dropped something else."

The girls started a search and presently Helen found a tiny envelope, farther under the chair. Nancy's name and address were typed on it!

"The charge plate must have been in this and slid out," she said. "My impersonator must have decided to type the envelope to be sure that she did not make a mistake when the clerks at Burk's Department Store asked for her address for the sales slips. I notice the letter *a* is faint."

Suddenly Nancy chuckled. "Em, you didn't want the police notified about the jewel theft, but here's a chance to get police help without telling them."

"How?"

"Chief McGinnis knows that my charge plate was stolen by an impersonator," Nancy answered. "With this typed clue, maybe he can find her. And I suspect that when he does, *your* thief will be caught!"

Nancy called Chief McGinnis at his home. She told him about the charge plate and envelope, and her suspicion that her impersonator, though not known to the inn's owners, must have been there.

"Please send the plate and envelope to me for

fingerprint analysis," Chief McGinnis requested.

Nancy promised she would and hung up, wishing she could have reported the jewel theft to him. It was after eleven o'clock when Helen and Nancy said good night to Emily and walked to their cottage. Both girls fell asleep almost as soon as their heads touched the pillows. But around three in the morning, Nancy was partially awakened by a noise.

"What was that?" she thought, looking around the cottage with sleepy eyes. She listened. But all was silent now. Finally Nancy went back to sleep.

She awoke at seven. Helen was still asleep. Nancy put on a casual sweater and skirt and loafers. She tiptoed from the cabin and headed for the inn. No one else seemed to be outside.

For the next half hour Nancy looked near the front door for footprints, lilac buds, or anything else to give her a clue to the jewel thief. She found nothing.

She strolled around back and met Hank, the gardener, who greeted her pleasantly and said he had decided not to give up his job. "My injured leg's better. But I have other worries now," he said. "Some outdoor equipment was taken last night from the tool shed."

"Really?" said Nancy. "What?"

Hank led her to the small wooden structure used by the outdoor workers. "We're missing several shovels, rakes, some wire, and small parts," said Hank. "But worst of all, an expensive jig saw that Mr. Farnham just bought is gone."

"More thefts," thought Nancy. Aloud she asked, "Is the shed locked at night?"

Hank said it was, and that he was responsible for securing the shed after work. "Probably none of the other men thought to ask Miss Willoughby for the spare key to lock up when I wasn't here."

Nancy examined the soft dirt outside the shed. There were a number of footprints, all blurred and leading in different directions. As Jim, Gil, and Luke—the three other gardeners—reported for work, Nancy questioned each of them in turn. They confessed that they had forgotten to lock the shed, and said they had no idea who might have taken the tools. Before Nancy left the men, she suggested that Hank search the grounds once more before reporting the theft.

As Nancy started up the front porch steps of the inn a few minutes later, she was hailed by John McBride. "Look what I found!" he cried triumphantly.

He held out Emily's white velvet jewel case!

CHAPTER VII

A Diver in Peril

"JOHN, you found the diamonds!" Nancy exclaimed.

The young man opened the case and displayed its contents. The twenty diamonds, of various sizes, glinted in the morning sunlight.

"Astounding, isn't it?" John grinned, adding that he had found the case under one of the lobby windows. "I must have missed it last night."

"Will you show me the spot, please? I must have missed it too."

John led Nancy to a clump of China-blue lilac bushes, and pointed out the place where he had found the case.

"The thief must have dropped this, but I can't figure out why she didn't come back for it," John remarked.

"She may not have known until later that she

had dropped it. By that time she probably was afraid of being caught," Nancy replied.

Just then Emily came outside. She was beside herself with joy upon seeing the jewels.

"John, you're a darling!" she cried. "Let's go to the patio and tell the others."

"Isn't this wonderful?" Mrs. Willoughby exclaimed. "And none of the diamonds is missing!" she added, counting.

"Are you sure?" Maud gave John and Nancy suspicious looks.

Nancy was about to make a sharp retort but refrained. The social director seemed determined to be unpleasant, and the young sleuth decided to ignore her insinuating remark. John just looked amused.

"Aunt Hazel," said Emily, "I think these jewels should be put in a safe place at once. Since I'm going to sell them, I think our jeweler friend in Benton, Mr. Fabian, is the person to keep them. And he can also make a new appraisal of the diamonds."

Emily's aunt nodded. "I'm so happy for you, dear."

Emily continued, "I might sell a few of the smaller diamonds today. We need cash immediately to take care of some outstanding bills."

Just then, Hank walked up to the group to tell Emily of the disappearance of the tools. The gardener asserted that he had conducted a thorough search.

An interested expression came over John's face and he said, "I'll search." Nancy wondered if anything unusual lay back of his offer.

Everyone went inside to breakfast. When the meal was finished, Mrs. Willoughby said to Emily, "I'd ride in to town with you, but I have a headache."

Emily insisted that her aunt rest. "Nancy and Helen will go with me, I'm sure."

The girls said they would be happy to. At once Maud asked if she might join the group. "All right," Emily said without enthusiasm.

Before they left, Nancy telephoned Hannah Gruen, reporting the loss and recovery of the diamonds and the finding of the charge plate. She chuckled. "Actually I'm out of a sleuthing job, Hannah, so I'll see you soon."

"But you haven't found out who your impersonator is," the housekeeper said. "She may keep on making trouble for you."

"You're right. I must find her. Now tell me about yourself."

The Drews' housekeeper reported an uneventful night and that a police guard was still posted at the house. "Your father wired he would be detained until tomorrow evening."

"Well, I'll be seeing you. 'Bye now.'"

On the ride to Benton, Nancy and Emily decided it was best not to mention to the jeweler the disappearance of her diamonds the previous night. "Even though I have them back, exaggerated stories might still get around."

When the group entered Fabian's Jewelry Store, Emily asked to see the owner. The pleasant-faced man greeted her cordially and was introduced to the other girls. Then Emily opened her jewel case.

"My, what a lovely collection of stones!" Mr. Fabian exclaimed.

He picked up a small diamond and studied it closely. Frowning, he put on his jeweler's eyepiece, examined the gem, then dropped it into the case. Diamond after diamond was scrutinized in this manner. Emily watched anxiously.

When Mr. Fabian put down the last gem he looked hard at Emily. "Is this a practical joke?" he asked. "These stones are only glass!"

Emily's face blanched. Helen and Maud were speechless.

Nancy was dismayed. Had the thief planted fake stones for some sinister purpose? "What is it?" she asked herself.

The jeweler was saying, "These are excellent imitations, Emily. Where did they come from?"

"Why—er—they were my mother's. I always thought they were real."

"I'm sorry," The jeweler smiled sympathetically, as he handed the case to Emily. Almost in a daze, she thanked him and the others followed her from the shop.

As they stood outside the store, Nancy and Helen tried to comfort their friend. "It's a shame," Helen said.

"It . . . it's the jinx again . . ." Emily sobbed. "I should have known. Oh, poor Dick! All our plans are spoiled."

"I'm not so sure," Nancy said. "I have a feeling the thief substituted these fakes for the real diamonds. I know it sounds funny . . ."

"Huh!" Maud exclaimed. Turning to Nancy, she said, "An awful lot of funny things have happened since you came to Lilac Inn."

"That's enough, Maud!" Emily brushed away her tears. "I won't have you insulting my friends. Anyway, maybe Nancy's right."

"Oh, I forgot. Nancy's a famous detective!" Maud said sarcastically.

Helen and Nancy kept still with difficulty. Nancy wondered why Maud had become so antagonistic toward her.

In silence, the four reached Nancy's car. As the others got in, Nancy stopped a newsboy to buy a River Heights morning paper. Nancy opened her change purse. Simultaneously, a woman coming from the opposite direction jostled Nancy's arm.

The purse dropped to the pavement, scattering change in every direction.

"Oh, bother!" Nancy exclaimed.

Emily jumped out of the car to help retrieve the money. A moment later she gave a startled cry and pointed to the ground.

Lying beside the ten-cent piece was a small diamond brilliantly reflecting the sunlight!

The expression on Nancy's face brought Helen and Maud hurrying from the car. Emily picked up the diamond.

"Is this yours, Nancy?" she asked.

"N—no, I never saw it before," Nancy stammered, completely astounded.

Maud looked smug. "Try and make anyone believe that. It's one of your diamonds, Emily!"

Nancy was too horrified to speak. Helen came to her friend's defense. Glaring at Maud, she declared, "If Nancy says she knows nothing about how the diamond got in her change purse, it's true!"

"Of course it is," Emily backed her up. "Oh Maud, why are you always so hateful?" Turning to Nancy, she said, "Someone has tried to throw suspicion on you. But why?"

"I don't know," Nancy replied. "If that's the case, I wonder if that woman who bumped me might be in league with the jewel thief." To herself she added, "Maybe my impersonator is trying to throw suspicion on me!"

She paid the boy for the paper, then asked him

and the others if they had noticed the woman. Unfortunately none of them had.

Nancy suggested that they have the new-found stone appraised, so the group re-entered Fabian's. The jeweler was surprised but obligingly put on his eyepiece.

"This is a perfect one-carat diamond!" he exclaimed. "If you're interested in selling, I'll be happy to make an offer."

"Not today, but I may be back." Emily smiled.

She and her friends returned to the convertible and Nancy headed for Lilac Inn. She speculated to herself on the imitation gems. "The thief learned the number and shapes of Emily's diamonds, and had the artificial ones made to match as closely as possible. Very clever."

Her thoughts were broken into by Maud asking Emily, "When are you going to tell Dick about the theft of your jewels?"

"When I get ready," was the cool reply.

As they turned into the Lilac Inn driveway, Emily sighed. "Aunt Hazel will be dreadfully upset to hear about the substitution of the gems."

"It'll put her to bed for a week," Maud prophesied unfeelingly. "Well, I'll see you all at lunch."

The noon meal was a rather uncomfortable one. Mrs. Willoughby was obviously dejected and ate little. Maud maintained an almost sulky silence. Nancy was preoccupied, though somewhat disappointed that John was not present. Also, a startling idea had come to her about the diamond in her purse: The noise which had awakened her during the night might have been made by an intruder leaving, perhaps by the bathroom window, after planting the diamond.

After luncheon Anna the waitress beckoned Nancy aside and handed her a note. "I just took this message from Mr. McBride on the phone. I was passing the desk and answered the ring."

Nancy thanked the girl and read the message. "Nancy: I've found an important clue to the case. Come in your canoe to the dock where you saw the man with the crew cut. Wear your diving gear."

Nancy was intrigued. What was John's discovery? What kind of clue would necessitate underwater equipment?

Since Maud was there, Nancy merely told the others she had a date with John, saying, "Dad warned me not to go anywhere alone, but if John's with me, I'll be safe." Nancy then hurried to put on her bathing suit. Over this she slipped her rubber insulation suit. Then, carrying mask, aqualung, flippers, and an underwater camera on a strap around her neck, she went to the dock.

Soon Nancy was paddling her canoe down the river, scanning the shore ahead for the place near which she and Helen had capsized. She finally sighted the dock where Helen had seen the man in the rowboat. On the bank nearby was a blue canoe with *Lilac Inn* painted on its side.

"John!" called Nancy, looking about. No answer. Again Nancy called his name. Silence.

A little distance beyond the dock the girl noticed a man fishing from the beach. He wore a wide-brimmed straw hat. Cupping her hands, Nancy called out and asked if he had seen the young man who had come in the canoe.

"Yeah," the fisherman yelled in a nasal voice. "He went underwater a couple of minutes ago— dived into the middle of the river opposite his canoe."

"Thanks." Nancy was mystified. Why hadn't John waited for her to arrive? He knew it was dangerous for anyone to go skin diving alone.

Hurriedly she beached her own craft, donned her mask and aqualung, and slipped on the flippers. Then she swam out to the middle of the river.

She made a quick dive to begin her descent. As she straightened out, Nancy kicked with her fins and propelled herself with her arms. The water became darker and cooler as she descended. Small fish flitted by. Presently Nancy realized she was nearing the bottom. She estimated that the river was about twenty feet deep at this spot.

When she reached the muddy floor, she glanced about in every direction. There was no sign of

John—only underwater plants and several large rocks.

Nancy swam cautiously and watched for crevices as she went forward. Every moment she expected to see John. Had he been underwater long? Had he met with a freak accident and been hurt? Even an expert skin diver can overestimate his physical abilities, she realized.

All of a sudden Nancy stopped abruptly. Her eyes widened and a chill went up her spine. Protruding from a massive rocky overhang was something that resembled a shark's head!

"It can't be!" she gasped inwardly. "Sharks don't live in fresh water!"

The sinister shape, however, was far too large to be an ordinary fish. Nancy's fear gave way to curiosity, as the object remained stationary. She inched forward, holding the camera in front of her and cocking the shutter. Three more strokes and she would have a good view of the mysterious form.

One—two— Nancy was about to shoot, when a slight movement in the water caused her to whirl around. A spear came hurtling from behind a big rock to Nancy's right. The next moment the tip of the spear lodged in the lens of her camera!

CHAPTER VIII

A Hoax Revealed

NANCY's heart thumped wildly as the spear quivered in her camera. Someone had tried to injure her! Why?

The girl detective's first instinct was to avoid further danger and rise to the surface as quickly as possible. But she paused to look around for the spear thrower. There was no sign of him.

"He may be getting ready for another attack, though," she thought. "I'd better not take a chance."

Gripping the camera, with the embedded spear, in both hands, she swam upward. At the surface, Nancy set out for shore and climbed to the dock. She glanced about for the fisherman, but he was not there.

Nancy removed her skin-diving gear, then examined the stainless-steel spear. It was the simplest type used for underwater fishing. The weapon was six feet long, with a sharp, thin tip.

Nancy shuddered as she pulled it from the lens of her camera.

"I'd better go back to the inn," she thought. "Dad was right about it being dangerous for me to be alone."

Nancy had been preoccupied with her narrow escape. Now she suddenly remembered John. To her astonishment, the Lilac Inn canoe was gone. Had John surfaced while Nancy was underwater, and, not seeing her, returned to the inn? Also, she wondered whether John was the skin diver seen by the fisherman on the river.

Nancy's head whirled with theories as she pushed her canoe into the water and stepped into it. Recalling the strange, sharklike object, she thought, "Perhaps the spear thrower didn't want me to photograph the object? And was that what John meant about a clue?"

As Nancy tied up at the inn dock, she saw that the blue canoe was there. "Well, anyway, he's back."

As the young sleuth headed for her cottage, she heard Helen call. Nancy stopped, and Helen, Emily, and Mrs. Willoughby hurried forward. They stared aghast at the spear in Nancy's hand.

"N-Nancy! You've been in danger!" Helen gasped.

Nancy gave a wry smile. Just then John McBride, dressed in slacks and sports shirt, hurried toward the group.

Before Nancy had a chance to question him, John exclaimed, "Fine thing, Nancy Drew! Standing me up to go skin diving!"

"Standing you up?" Nancy retorted. "Where were you?"

"In the apple orchard," John replied. "Waiting for you, where I said I'd be."

Nancy shook her head. "There's been a horrible mix-up. I'll tell my story first."

When she had finished, John and the others expressed amazement and concern.

"Nancy," the young man said, "I didn't phone any message to you. Someone else did, apparently to keep you from seeing me in the orchard."

"What's all this about the orchard?" Nancy demanded.

John reminded her that at eleven o'clock she had hailed him from the patio. "I had just returned after failing to find the missing tools. You were wearing the pink dress you had on the night before. You said you had something to discuss with me, and asked if I would meet you at twelve-thirty in the apple orchard. I said I'd be glad to."

"Why, I was in Benton at eleven o'clock!" Nancy exclaimed. "I wasn't the girl you talked to!"

John looked dumfounded. "But the girl sounded and looked exactly like you." He added that he had taken a sandwich with him to the orchard, but left at one-thirty, deciding that Nancy had changed her mind.

Emily caught her breath. "Oh, Nancy! It must have been the girl who is impersonating you!"

John nodded somberly. "I'm afraid so. I sure was fooled. And someone wanted to get you away from here and even harm you, perhaps fatally!"

Helen looked distressed, and Mrs. Willoughby wrung her hands. "We must report all this to the police immediately. No one at Lilac Inn is safe."

Emily, though concerned, still held back. "Please—not until Dick gets home tomorrow. In the meantime, Nancy may solve the mystery."

Her aunt reluctantly agreed. Nancy had been silent, trying to fit the various elements of the puzzle together. It was evident to her that her "twin" had firsthand knowledge as to where she and others at the inn would be at certain times. Nancy was certain the girl's actions further indicated accomplices, and dangerous ones at that, judging from the spear thrower. Offhand, Nancy could not imagine anyone at the inn being involved in such scheming, not even Maud.

"Has anything else been stolen?" she asked abruptly.

"I haven't heard of any losses," Emily replied.

"What's the next move, Detective Drew?" Helen spoke up.

"I'm not sure," Nancy replied thoughtfully. "But I do agree, for the time being, it would be best not to have the police investigate either the river or the inn. Since our enemies apparently want me out of the way, it must mean they want to stay here. Let's hope we can catch them before they decide to leave!"

John changed the subject. "I'd like to investigate the place in the river where you saw that 'shark,' Nancy. Also, I'll try to find out who used the inn's canoe. See you later."

Nancy returned to her cottage. She put away the skin-diving gear and set the spear in the closet.

"I'd better hang on to this for evidence, even though there probably aren't any fingerprints on it except mine."

She took out her pink dress. It looked crisp and fresh.

"My impersonator sure is a quick-change artist," Nancy thought. "She must have let herself into the cottage while I was in Benton, and returned the dress while I was at lunch.

"I'd better lock every window and put a padlock on the door," she determined, selecting a green cotton dress to wear, "and also make some inquiries around here. Maybe someone saw a girl enter this cabin."

A newspaper Helen had bought that morning lay on a table. Absently Nancy looked at the first page. Suddenly her eyes widened. With interest she read a report about a red panel truck having been stolen two days before.

"An identifying mark," she read further, "is a chrome eagle ornament on the hood. The truck is believed to be in the vicinity of Benton."

Was this the truck which had forced her car into the ditch? Lieutenant Brice must have pursued her lead, and found out that the vehicle had been stolen.

"No wonder the driver was in such a hurry!" Nancy thought as she left the cottage.

On the way to join the others, Nancy had a sudden hunch. Mary Mason had left the inn abruptly, with the flimsy excuse that the place was haunted. "I never pursued that lead," the young sleuth told herself. "Anna was here then. Maybe she knows where Mary Mason is."

Before joining her friends, Nancy hurried to the kitchen to talk to Anna. The waitress was not there. A strange girl came up to her, and introduced herself as Jean Holmes. Jean's complexion was very pale, and her brown hair thick and combed close to her face. She wore heavy glasses.

"Can I help you?" she asked, smiling shyly.

Nancy inquired where Anna was. Jean said she had gone to the storage cellar. Nancy went downstairs and found Anna bringing out a supply of preserved fruits and jellies.

"Anna," Nancy said, "I'm trying to locate Mary Mason who used to work here. Do you know her home address?"

Anna shook her head, but said she would inquire among the other waitresses who had been there when Mary was.

"Thank you," said Nancy, and went to join her group on the patio.

She noticed that Maud Potter was not present. At the first opportunity, she asked Helen about this.

"Oh, Maud's been very exclusive. She stayed in her room all afternoon." Helen added dryly, "She hasn't been missed."

Maud did show up later and went to the dining room with the group. Nancy asked John if he had been rewarded in his sleuthing.

He shook his head. "I saw no 'sharks,' and no one here admits to having used the canoe."

This reminded Nancy of the fisherman she had seen on the river. Because of his hat, she had not been able to tell if his hair was crew cut. But she wondered if he might be the man Helen had seen after the girls' canoe had capsized.

At the supper table Nancy confided this idea to her friend in a low tone. Helen wrinkled her brow. "From the general impression I had of Mr. Crew Cut, Nancy, he could be the same one. But of course I only saw him from a distance."

Both girls became aware that Maud was eying them closely. "Planning another skin-diving excursion, Nancy?" the woman asked sarcastically.

Mrs. Willoughby hurriedly put in, "Oh, yes. I told Maud the latest—er—troubles."

"I should hope so!" Maud said sharply. "If there are dangerous people lurking around here, I'd like to be warned."

"Nancy's the one in danger," Emily reminded Maud coldly.

To change the subject, Nancy observed, "The new waitress, Jean Holmes, seems to be very efficient."

Maud tossed her head. "I do have an instinct about people, you know." But she was clearly pleased at Nancy's remark.

After supper Nancy was leaving the room with the others when Anna came up behind her. "I have some information for you, Miss Drew," the waitress whispered. "Mary Mason mostly kept to herself, but Kitty, one of the girls, thinks Mary commuted to Dockville every night. She also remembers that Mary once worked for a Mrs. Ernest Stonewell in River Heights."

"You're very helpful, Anna," Nancy said. "Thank you."

Nancy went to the hall desk and picked up a telephone directory. There were several Masons listed in Dockville, which was near River Heights. The young sleuth dialed the number of each Mason. Nobody knew Mary, the waitress. Nancy now looked up Mrs. Ernest Stonewell's address.

"I'll call her tomorrow."

The rest of the evening Nancy spent playing a lively game of ping-pong with Helen, Emily, and

John. Around eleven o'clock everyone said good night. John walked with the two girls to their cottage and warned them to secure the new inside bolt on the door, as well as the bathroom window. "I'm within calling distance if you need me." He smiled.

"Thanks, John," said Nancy. "Every window sill in the bedroom will have a book on it. If any intruder tries getting in, I hope he won't notice the book, and will knock it off and wake us!"

Before going to sleep, Nancy thought happily that her father would soon be home. How much she had to tell him!

Helen, in the meantime, was wide awake. She tossed and turned restlessly. Finally, at midnight, she got up and put on her bathrobe and slippers.

"Maybe some fresh air will help me sleep," Helen thought.

Despite John's warning, she slid the bolt and left the cottage, closing the door quietly. The grounds were dark and silent. Helen turned toward the lilac grove.

Suddenly she saw a flickering light ahead, near the grove. Curious, she drew closer. A veiled figure with black hair and wearing a glowing white gown confronted her. The next instant Helen was struck on the back of her head and fell unconscious!

CHAPTER IX

The Search

BACK in the cottage, Nancy was awakened by an insistent ticking. She sat up and glanced in annoyance at her alarm clock. It certainly seemed noisy.

Suddenly Nancy realized that her friend's bed was empty. "Helen?" she called, thinking that perhaps the other girl had gone to get a glass of water. There was no reply.

"Where can Helen be at one-thirty in the morning?" Nancy asked herself. Hurriedly she put on robe and slippers and picked up her flashlight. When she found the front door of the cottage unbolted, she felt a pang of alarm.

Outside, Nancy searched the cottage area, calling her friend's name again and again. No response. Finally, thoroughly alarmed, Nancy decided to ask John for help. She knocked on his door. No answer. Perplexed, Nancy was about to leave when a twig crackled a short distance away. She turned off her flashlight and crouched behind a low shrub. Who was approaching? She was relieved a moment later to discern the familiar outline of John.

"Oh, thank goodness!" Nancy exclaimed, hurrying toward him. "Have you seen Helen?" she asked. "I woke up and found her gone."

"No, I haven't seen her," John replied. "I couldn't sleep so I walked down the road. Come on. We'll both look."

They started across the lawn.

"Let's check the inn first," Nancy proposed. "Maybe Helen's there."

The grounds seemed eerie in the moonless night as the couple walked quietly, beaming their flashes ahead of them. They circled the inn. The place was completely dark, with the exception of the tiny night light in the main lobby.

Nancy suggested they try all the doors. "If one is unlocked, it may mean Helen is inside."

The front, rear, patio, and kitchen doors were securely bolted from the inside.

"Perhaps Helen couldn't sleep and went for a walk near the river," John suggested.

Quickly he and Nancy went to the waterfront. Starting with the area near the dock, they proceeded along the bank, calling Helen's name. As they came to the lilac grove, John said:

"I don't think—"

He was interrupted by a low moan which came from beyond a lilac bush. The couple hurried toward it, with Nancy focusing the beam of her flashlight on the ground.

"Helen!" she exclaimed in horror.

Before them lay her friend, unconscious.

Quickly Nancy and John knelt beside Helen. John held the flashlight while Nancy made a rapid examination. Helen's pulse was normal, but there was an ugly lump on the back of her head.

John looked grim as Nancy chafed Helen's wrists. "She must have been struck by a blunt instrument," he said.

Helen's eyelids flickered open. For a moment the girl looked terrified, then smiled feebly as she recognized John and Nancy.

"Wh-what happened?" she murmured.

"Don't talk," Nancy said soothingly, but Helen insisted upon sitting up.

"Oh, my head!" she groaned, and leaned against Nancy.

A few minutes later the injured girl was able to talk. She explained about leaving the cabin and walking toward the lilac grove, then told of the strange figure in white she had seen.

Helen described the long translucent robe the figure had worn. "The last thing I saw was that ghostly figure waving her arms back and forth, as if signaling to someone. Then I was struck on the head and blacked out."

"Don't talk any more now," said John, as Helen sighed wearily. "We'll go back to the cottage and Nancy will put you to bed."

John carried Helen, and with Nancy's guiding light, headed toward the cottage. They had hardly started when the trio was startled by a loud *boo-oo-m!* It seemed to come from the direction of the cottages!

"That sounded like an explosion!" cried Nancy. She broke into a run.

John, carrying Helen, followed as fast as he could. A moment later Nancy heard a crackling noise and smelled smoke.

"John!" Nancy cried in horror. "Look! Our cottage is on fire!"

The young people stared ahead in dismay. Tongues of orange-red flames were indeed shooting upward from the girls' cottage! The trio could already feel the heat from the blaze.

"We'll have to douse it," John said tensely. "The whole row will burn down if we wait for the fire department."

Helen insisted she was strong enough to walk. "I can help!"

John raced to the side of the inn where an extension water hose was attached. "Get the buckets near the kitchen door!" he shouted to the girls.

They dashed toward the inn. At the same time, the hall lights came on and the front door was flung open. Emily, Maud, and Mrs. Willoughby, dressed in robes, rushed out. Behind them was Mr. Daly, carrying a Revolutionary War musket!

Each group was amazed to see the other but Nancy took no time asking questions. "Our cottage is on fire!" she announced.

Soon everyone joined in tossing bucket after bucket of water from a garden spigot onto the blaze. John played a steady stream from the hose. Gradually the blaze was reduced to embers.

"Glad we saved the other units, anyhow," John said, glancing at the ruined guest cottage. "Too bad you girls lost all your clothes."

"But saved our lives by not being in the cottage," Nancy remarked grimly.

"How did the fire start? What caused that explosion?" Emily asked, explaining that she and the others had been awakened by the noise.

"I believe," Nancy said gravely, "it was caused by a time bomb which someone placed in our cottage before we went to bed. A ticking sound woke me. I thought it was my clock."

Her listeners were shocked. Mrs. Willoughby grew deathly pale, as Maud shrilled, "There must be a lunatic loose around here."

For once Nancy was inclined to agree with her. The young sleuth added that of course nothing could be determined until daylight when the ruins would be examined.

The exhausted group went back to the inn. "Nancy and Helen," Emily said, "I feel terrible about this whole thing."

Mrs. Willoughby, too, expressed her regret. "At least some of the loss will be covered by our fire insurance," she added.

Nancy smiled and nodded, then started to relate Helen's startling experience just before the fire.

When Nancy came to the part about the woman in the white robe, Emily shivered. "I don't believe in ghosts," she averred, "but Mary Mason probably saw this person. That's why she said Lilac Inn was haunted!"

Nancy suddenly noticed how pale Helen was and suggested she get to bed at once.

"Oh, yes," said Emily. "Nancy and Helen, take the front second-floor bedroom."

Nancy noticed that Mr. Daly still clutched the ancient musket. With a sheepish smile, he said, "Shortly before the explosion, I thought I heard someone prowling around outside. I grabbed this old musket—guess it's been here since the inn was built. It's not loaded, but I figured it might scare away an intruder."

John grinned. "Nancy and I were your 'prowlers.'" He explained that they had tried all the doors in their search for Helen.

The women and girls started upstairs. John and Mr. Daly, carrying his musket, said they would "stand guard" for the rest of the night.

As Emily showed Nancy and Helen to their room, she said firmly, "This awful experience has made me decide to call the police first thing in the morning!"

"Oh, Emily, thank goodness!" Helen exclaimed in relief. "If there *is* some kind of maniac loose at Lilac Inn, you'll be doing the right thing."

Emily stepped closer to the girls. "When the police arrive," she whispered, "I'd appreciate it if you still don't mention the diamond theft."

Her friends, though surprised, promised not to say a word about it.

"You see," Emily went on softly, "it's not for my sake, but Aunt Hazel's. I can't explain any more right now. You go to bed. I'll call you if I need you."

Nancy and Helen were too polite to ask further questions. Nevertheless, Nancy fell asleep wondering about Emily's request. When the young sleuth awoke in the morning, her first thought was of the bomb. When had it been planted? While she was skin diving?

"The person who placed the bomb might have been seen by someone connected with the inn," Nancy speculated.

Helen awoke just then, and Nancy asked how she felt. "Fine, except for a slight headache." Helen shuddered. "Last night seems like a terrible dream!"

A few minutes later Emily knocked on the door with clothes for Helen and Nancy to borrow. While they dressed, she reported that a trooper from the Benton State Police Barracks would be over shortly to inspect the burned cottage.

"John checked the lilac grove at daybreak," she added. "There were lots of footprints of various sizes, but no sign of any suspicious person."

"Maybe I *was* dreaming I saw the ghost," Helen said. She felt the back of her head. "But this bump is real!"

The three girls went down to breakfast. John, Mrs. Willoughby, and Maud were already at the table. No other guests were in the room. Nancy gave her order to Anna.

At a nearby table the waitress Jean Holmes was arranging flowers in a copper vase. The girl smiled shyly at Nancy, picked up the bowl, and walked toward the bay window. As she started to place the flowers on the wide sill, Jean gave a startled cry. She dropped the bowl, scattering flowers and water on the floor.

Everyone at the table stared out the window. Two men were peering in. Nancy recognized them and jumped to her feet in surprise.

CHAPTER X

"Blue Pipes"

THE unexpected sight of the two men peering through the dining-room window had startled Nancy, but in a happy way. She recognized the observers as her father and the state trooper, Lieutenant Brice.

As Jean apologized for her clumsiness and went to the kitchen for her broom and mop, Nancy hurried to the hall. She greeted her tall, handsome father and the officer who had come to her rescue when her car was forced into the ditch.

"Nancy, are you all right?" was Carson Drew's first question.

"Oh, just fine, Dad. What a nice surprise to see you!" She kissed him affectionately. With a smile she added, "I didn't expect to see you again so soon, Lieutenant Brice."

The officer grinned. He explained that he had been assigned to investigate the cottage fire.

When he arrived at Lilac Inn, he had met Carson Drew, who had just driven up. The two men were completing a quick tour of the grounds when they passed the dining room and looked in.

Mr. Drew chuckled. "I thought I'd surprise you, Nancy, but I didn't expect to scare that waitress."

"So many upsetting things have happened here, Dad," Nancy said, "I guess everyone's a bit nervous."

Mr. Drew said that until he had met the officer in the parking lot, he had heard nothing of the trouble at Lilac Inn.

"The lieutenant mentioned last night's explosion and fire here. Then he asked if I were the father of the Nancy Drew who had the accident on the side road to Benton."

"You haven't talked to Hannah?" Nancy asked.

"No. I came directly here." Mr. Drew put an arm around his daughter. "I'm concerned about you."

"I'm all right, Dad," Nancy insisted. "Really I am. By the way, have you talked to Chief Mc-Ginnis?"

"Yes. That's another reason I came here," her father said. "I had to phone him on a legal matter. He told me that you found the charge plate and the envelope with your name on it. By the way, there were no helpful prints on either the plate or the envelope."

Nancy decided to wait before telling her father of the other mysterious incidents, and now suggested that the men come into the dining room to breakfast. She made the necessary introductions. The Willoughbys and Mr. Drew were well acquainted and exchanged warm greetings.

Maud fluttered her eyelashes. "So *you're* the famous criminal lawyer," she said coyly.

Carson Drew did not like flattery, but nodded politely. He congratulated Emily on her forthcoming marriage. When the men had finished eating, Nancy and her friends went with them to see the burned cottage.

Emily told Lieutenant Brice everything that had happened but excluded the diamond theft. He rubbed his chin thoughtfully, then said, "All could be malicious pranks, not connected with the explosion. On the other hand, they could very well be part of some big scheme."

When the group reached the site of the burned cottage, they found John there. Nancy introduced him to her father and the police officer.

After Lieutenant Brice had probed the ruins of the cottage, Nancy and her friends gave him and Mr. Drew a full account of the previous night's events. When he heard of Helen's experience, Mr. Drew looked grave and suggested she return home.

Helen shook her head. "I can't desert Nancy."

The young sleuth smiled gratefully. Secretly

she longed to tell her father the rest of the story—the trip to Benton, the diamond turning up in her purse, the faked message from John, and her skindiving adventure. But all these, Nancy realized, were related to Emily's stolen gems.

Finally Lieutenant Brice announced, "I've found fragments of what I am positive *was* a time bomb you heard ticking, Miss Drew. I'll send an explosives expert over to verify this, however."

Carson Drew turned to his daughter. "Nancy, I wish I could stay here and help you work out this mystery. Unfortunately, I have to return to River Heights and review highly important evidence for a case I'm to try next week. But keep me posted."

"I will, Dad. In fact, I may see you if I do some sleuthing near home, as I plan."

Before leaving, Mr. Drew asked if Nancy had come upon any leads to her impersonator.

"Nothing definite, Dad," was all Nancy could in truth reply.

The attorney then advised Emily to engage a guard to stand night duty. "I can recommend an excellent man," he said. "His name is Carl Bard."

Emily agreed and Mr. Drew went inside the inn to telephone him. He returned shortly and said Mr. Bard would report there later.

"Fine," said Lieutenant Brice. "And I'll have a squad car patrol the inn frequently. I suggest that no one venture out alone—especially at night—until this case is broken."

Good-bys were exchanged, and Nancy stood waving to her father as he drove off. Meanwhile, Helen and Emily had started for the patio.

As Nancy hurried after them, she came to the tool shed. John had investigated it, but Nancy wondered if she might find some clue he had overlooked.

The door was open. She went inside. Spades, hoes, rakes, and other similar equipment lined the walls. Nancy studied the array. "Just ordinary garden tools," she mused. Then suddenly she noticed a pad of notepaper lying on a bench. Nancy picked it up and turned the pages, which contained various notations for the gardeners. One item, on the third page and in a different kind of printing from the other instructions, read: "Prune blue pipes near grove."

" 'Blue pipes,' " thought Nancy, as she tore out the sheet. "Now what does that mean? Could it possibly be a code message? Or a signal? I'll ask the gardeners."

She left the shed, and began to look for the men. The only man in sight was Gil, who was cutting the lawn with a power mower. She went up, and attracting his attention, asked him, "Can you tell me what 'blue pipes' are?"

"Never heard of 'em," Gil replied laconically.

"One more question," Nancy said. "Would you have any idea who used one of the inn's canoes yesterday afternoon?"

For a moment Gil's eyes narrowed. Then he brusquely replied No; he had not been near the dock all day. "Mr. John asked me the same thing. Well, I got work to do," he muttered, and quickly resumed his mowing.

Nancy walked meditatively toward the inn. "If Gil doesn't know what 'blue pipes' are, that message might well be a code phrase."

It occurred to her that perhaps Mr. Daly would be able to explain the term. Nancy went inside and found the elderly gentleman in his office, going over receipts. He looked up as she knocked and entered.

"Good morning, Nancy. Sorry I missed meeting your father."

Mr. Daly admitted that he had been wearied by his all-night vigil, and had gone to his room to rest. Nancy smiled understandingly and told him briefly of Lieutenant Brice's investigation.

Mr. Daly looked grave. "If all this danger continues, I'm going to insist that Emily and Dick sell the inn. A nice young couple shouldn't start marriage under such circumstances."

"I agree. But the person responsible for the trouble here must be caught."

"You're right, Nancy," Mr. Daly said. "I mustn't lose hope so easily."

The young sleuth then asked, "Mr. Daly, can you tell me what 'blue pipes' are?"

Mr. Daly chuckled. "Of course—my favorite subject matter is 'blue pipes'—or lilacs."

"You mean that 'blue pipes' are lilacs?" Nancy inquired with interest.

"Yes. The ancient name of the lilac was Blue Pipe Tree, a reminder of the time when pipes were made of its wood. See here."

Mr. Daly reached into a drawer of his desk and handed Nancy a half-finished tobacco pipe. "Carving is my hobby. I'm making this pipe from the wood of a fallen tree limb right here at Lilac Inn."

"Why, it's beautiful!" Nancy held up the pipe, admiring the delicate stem.

At that moment Jean Holmes passed the office. She paused and looked in. Nancy greeted her, but the waitress barely answered. Her eyes were riveted on the pipe in Nancy's hand.

"Isn't this a handsome piece, Jean?" Nancy said pleasantly. "Mr. Daly made it."

"Oh, very." Jean nodded and hastened on into the dining room.

To Nancy it seemed that the waitress had acted almost frightened. Why?

Mr. Daly seemed not to have noticed. He went on to tell Nancy some interesting facts about lilacs. The old-fashioned, lavender-colored blossom and its white companion, so well known in America, originally came from Bulgaria, Hungary, and Rumania. But the double lilacs of pink, red, and purple, like those in the grove, were developed by horticulturists.

"The French developed the Lucie Baltet variety—the same as the stolen tree," Mr. Daly said sadly. "Many beautiful lilacs are named after famous French people, such as Joan of Arc."

"You're certainly an expert on every aspect of lilacs," Nancy complimented him as Mr. Daly paused.

Modestly, Mr. Daly admitted he had studied the subject intensively. He himself had planted most of the lilacs at the inn.

"They are considered a flower of mysterious power in the West Indies," he said solemnly. "Some people there believe that the perfume keeps away ghosts and evil spirits. A lilac tree is often planted near the front door so its branches can act as protection against evil spirits entering the house."

Nancy now pulled the sheet with the blue pipe notation from her pocket and passed it to Mr. Daly. "Do you know anything about this?" she asked.

He glanced at it and said, "No. And I write out all the instructions for the gardeners. I never use the term 'blue pipes.' They wouldn't know what it meant."

"Have you any idea who might have written this?" Nancy asked.

"None whatever. And I can't figure out what it means. Besides, it's not time to prune lilacs. Have you a theory?"

"I'm not sure, except I have a hunch it's connected with the strange happenings at Lilac Inn and is a code message. I hope I can figure it out."

Nancy pocketed the sheet and left the office. Deep in thought, she almost bumped into Emily.

"Oh, where's Detective Drew headed?"

The young sleuth laughed, then showed Emily the sheet. "Do you know who printed this strange notation?"

Emily stared at the message for several seconds. Finally she said, "No, but the printing looks familiar."

"Think hard and don't keep any secrets," Nancy urged. "This may be the turning point in solving the mystery!"

Staring into space, Emily sought desperately for an answer. Suddenly she snapped her fingers. "I have it! That waitress who left here so suddenly! She used to print all the orders she took. I mean *Mary Mason!*"

CHAPTER XI

A Tip from a Waitress

"MARY MASON again!" exclaimed Nancy. "That settles it! I'm going to River Heights at once and talk to Mrs. Ernest Stonewell, the woman for whom she used to work."

Nancy decided to tell Helen her plan, so the two girls went out to the patio where she was reading. Nancy revealed her latest findings and told of her proposed trip. "Want to come?" she asked Helen.

"No, thanks." Helen chuckled. "You work better alone. What a clue this is! Maybe you'll come back with the mystery solved!"

"Don't count on that." Nancy smiled. "Where is everybody?"

"John's at the burned cottage with the explosives expert. Mrs. Willoughby and Maud are upstairs."

Nancy leaned toward Emily and said in a low voice, "I hope you won't mind my asking, but—

but does Maud Potter have anything to do with your not reporting the diamond theft?"

Emily sighed. "Well, yes. You've probably sensed, Nancy, that she seems to have some influence over Aunt Hazel."

Helen's eyes grew wide. "You mean Maud's sort of—blackmailing her?"

The bride-to-be looked unhappy. "I'm really not sure."

"And," Nancy conjectured, "you're afraid Maud has some knowledge of the diamonds that may involve your aunt if the theft is publicized?"

"That's the feeling I have."

Before the girls could discuss the matter further, Maud herself came onto the patio. She sank into a chair. "Having a conference?" she asked sweetly.

"Yes," Emily replied promptly. "Nancy's going on a sleuthing trip to River Heights."

"Oh?" Maud's eyelids flickered. "You have what they call a 'hot clue'?" she asked Nancy.

"I hope so," replied the young sleuth calmly.

"Well, give my regards to your dad if you see him," Maud said airily.

Nancy rose. "I'd better get started. I'll pick up more clothes for you and me, Helen." She laughed. "Then we can return yours, Em."

Suddenly the group became aware that Jean Holmes, dressed in street clothes, stood in the doorway. She smiled timidly and said:

"Miss Drew, I heard you say that you're going to River Heights. I need a few things I left in the room I shared in town with a girl friend." She turned to Emily, and asked permission to accompany Nancy and get them.

"All right," Emily said. "I trust you'll return in time to serve supper?"

"Oh, yes, Miss Willoughby. I'll take the afternoon bus back."

Nancy told Emily she herself probably would be back by evening.

"We'll be on pins and needles until then," Helen said.

Just before Nancy and Jean reached the convertible, Emily caught up to them. Drawing Nancy aside, she whispered, "I've been thinking —will you tell your father about my diamonds and the other incidents? Perhaps he can give you helpful advice. But please ask him to say nothing to the police, unless there's no other way out."

Nancy was delighted. She would feel much better if she could discuss this aspect of the case with her father.

In a few minutes she and Jean were headed for River Heights. Although Nancy had lost her handbag with wallet and driver's license in the fire, Mr. Drew had obtained special permission for her to drive until her new license was mailed. Fortunately, he had had a key to her car in his key case, and had left it with her.

"This is a lovely convertible," Jean spoke up.

Nancy smiled as the car rode smoothly past farm land and woods. "Where did you work before coming to Lilac Inn, Jean?" she asked.

"Many different places," the girl replied. "Florida in the winter, sometimes, and in the summer, I come north."

Later, as they neared River Heights, the waitress said abruptly:

"Miss Drew, I had another reason for asking to ride with you. I wanted to tell you someone at the inn is trying to make trouble for you!"

"What do you mean?" Nancy asked, as they reached the outskirts of River Heights.

Jean hesitated at first, then said she didn't want to be accused of spying. "I think," she said finally, "Mrs. Potter is up to something funny!"

"Why?"

Jean revealed that twice she had seen Maud going into Nancy's room—yesterday, at the cottage, and then at the inn that morning.

"Really?" Nancy tried to appear nonchalant. "At what times?"

Jean was vague. She said that she had arrived at the inn shortly before lunch the previous day. "I was unpacking in my room," Jean went on. "I looked out the window and saw Mrs. Potter enter your cottage.

"This morning," she continued, "I was at the second-floor linen closet when I heard footsteps.

I looked down the hall in time to see Mrs. Potter lock your door."

Nancy's mind raced. Was Maud directly implicated in the strange happenings at the inn? For what purpose had she entered the girls' rooms? It struck Nancy as odd, however, that Jean would inform on the woman who had helped her obtain a job. To the waitress she merely said, "Thank you for telling me."

"You and Miss Corning were lucky that you weren't hurt in the cottage fire," Jean remarked.

"Yes, very lucky," Nancy replied. Evidently Emily had said nothing to the servants about a bomb being the real cause of the blaze.

Nancy asked Jean if she had ever met a girl named Mary Mason from Dockville. "Mary used to work at the inn."

Jean wrinkled her brow. "No, although the name is familiar. Perhaps I once met a Miss Mason at one of the places I've worked."

They were now entering the business section of River Heights. Jean asked Nancy to let her off in the center of town. "I'm going to the optician's first. Then I'll go to my girl friend's."

Nancy stopped near Burk's Department Store. Jean thanked her profusely and got out. The young sleuth drove to a nearby tearoom for a quick snack. Then she continued on to Meadowbrook Lane, in an attractive residential section, where Mrs. Stonewell lived. Nancy soon spotted the number and stopped in front of an imposing Tudor-style home.

She hurried up to the front entrance and rang the doorbell. A maid answered. Nancy gave her name and asked to see Mrs. Stonewell. The caller was requested to take a seat in the living room.

A few minutes later Mrs. Stonewell, attractively dressed in a tailored sports suit, stepped into the room. With a gracious smile, she asked, "Is there something I can do for you, Miss Drew?"

"Yes, Mrs. Stonewell. I'm trying to trace a girl named Mary Mason," Nancy explained. "I understand she worked for you."

The woman's smile vanished. "Let's say I hired her. But I didn't get much work from Mary Mason. I discharged her after a month." She glanced at Nancy curiously. "*You* don't want to hire her?"

"Oh, no," Nancy replied. "She has some information I need. Do you know Mary's home address?"

"No. She lived in while working for me," said Mrs. Stonewell. "I do remember she occasionally visited a brother in Dockville. Whether or not she is living there, I can't say. Nor do I know the street address."

"One more question," Nancy said. "Did you ever miss anything while Mary was working for you?"

"Not that I know of."

Nancy thanked Mrs. Stonewell and departed.

She decided that when she returned to Lilac Inn later that day she would go by way of Dockville. Her next stop was at Helen's house. Nancy reassured Mrs. Corning, who had read about the fire, of Helen's well-being.

"Nancy," Mrs. Corning said, "the newspaper didn't state how the fire started. I suppose the usual carelessness—someone tossing away a lighted match."

Nancy, inwardly relieved, replied that this was always a possibility. She did not mention the time bomb.

With additional clothes for Helen in her car, Nancy drove home. She found that Mr. Drew was out for the afternoon in connection with his case.

When Hannah heard Nancy's account of the fire, she exclaimed, "Even on a pleasure trip, Nancy, danger follows you!" She looked at the girl knowingly. "And what about this twin of yours? Has she followed you to Lilac Inn?"

"Hannah, you're becoming a detective," Nancy accused fondly. "Seriously," she added, "you guessed it. She even managed to fool a friend of Emily's fiancé who's staying out there. But she vanished again."

Hannah sighed. "I'll certainly be glad when she's caught."

"I hope to do that soon," Nancy stated. "After I pack some clothes, I'm going sleuthing in Dockville." She explained about tracing Mary Mason.

"That's a terrible place," Hannah cried worriedly. "Oh, dear, I'd better go with you."

"Don't worry," said Nancy. "I'll be safe in the daylight. When Dad gets back, please tell him where I've gone."

Nancy quickly packed a suitcase. She also took along her spare set of skin-diving gear. Then, before leaving, she wrote her father a note telling the details of the jewelry theft.

When she reached Dockville later, Nancy glanced about in dismay. She was confronted with row upon row of dingy tenements. In which one did the suspect's brother live?

Nancy stopped her convertible and inquired of a stout woman where she could find a family by the name of Mason. The woman shook her head, evidently not understanding English.

"I'll try another block," Nancy decided, and turned into a winding narrow street which led along the river front.

She decided to inquire again and pulled up to the curb. She was about to alight when she glanced in the rear-view mirror. Directly behind her was a red panel truck. It looked exactly like the stolen vehicle which had forced her off the road. No one was in it, but the motor was running. Nancy turned her head to get a better look at the truck.

At the same moment she saw a large rock hurtling through the air toward her open window!

CHAPTER XII

A Daring Plan

BANG! The rock struck the door of Nancy's convertible, just as she ducked down. When Nancy cautiously raised her head a few seconds later, she looked all around to see if she could spot the rock thrower. No one was in sight.

Nancy glanced into the rear-view mirror again. The red truck had disappeared! Had the truck driver thrown the rock? If it had struck her, she would have been badly injured. A peculiar coincidence, at the least, Nancy thought.

Quickly Nancy climbed out and examined her car door. The rock had made a dent, but there was no further damage. She determined to continue her search for Mary Mason, and hailed a grocer's delivery truck which was coming down the street. When she asked the driver if he had seen the red truck, the man said No.

"Do you know where I might find someone here by the name of Mason?" Nancy inquired.

"Yes. Bud Mason. He lives in the next block, on Sixth Street," the man replied. "I've made deliveries there. It's number 12."

Nancy thanked him. She drove along the river, and turned left on Sixth Street. The houses here were in better condition than the others she had seen in Dockville. Number twelve was a white cottage with flowers bordering the front path.

When Nancy rang the bell, the door was opened by a red-haired woman of about thirty-five. She had clear-cut features and wore heavy make-up. She wore a snug-fitting lavender dress.

Nancy introduced herself and said she was looking for a Miss Mary Mason who had worked at Lilac Inn.

"You've come to the right address," the woman replied. "I'm Mary. Come in."

"Thank you." Nancy entered a room furnished with comfortable leather furniture, books, and several pictures of nautical scenes.

The woman eyed her caller curiously. She invited Nancy to sit down and asked, "What brings you here?"

Nancy explained that she was a friend of Emily Willoughby and was visiting at Lilac Inn.

"Miss Willoughby tells me you left because the inn was haunted," Nancy went on. "Since then, she's been wondering what you meant. I said I'd try to find you and ask."

Mary had listened attentively. Now she gave a high-pitched giggle. "So Miss Willoughby's getting scared. It's true—Lilac Inn *is* haunted!"

Mary proceeded to give Nancy a dramatic story of hearing footsteps at night when no one was around. She said that several times when she had been working late in the kitchen, a ghostly face had looked in the window.

"It's a spooky old place!" Mary shuddered. "I don't know how I stood it—the grounds are so lonely and creepy at night. Besides, commuting to my brother's here was too long a trip."

Nancy wondered if she were on the wrong track, after all. Perhaps Mary had left because of fright, and had wanted merely to find work closer to town.

The young sleuth looked around. "This is a pleasant home," she said. "Have you always lived with your brother?"

Mary answered readily, "No, just since I returned to Dockville, two months ago. I worked down South during the winter, and before that, out West. I hadn't seen Bud for a couple of years. When I came back here, he suggested I get a job nearby."

She paused. "Say, Miss Drew, how did you know I was in Dockville?"

Nancy explained about her call on Mrs. Stonewell.

Mary scowled. "That fuss-budget wanted a slave, not a maid. I was glad when she fired me."

Mary went on to say that after she left Lilac Inn, she had stayed here. "I'm keeping house for Bud until I find a really good deal."

"Oh—by the way," Nancy said casually, "the other day I found a note to the gardeners. I understand you printed it."

For a fraction of a second Nancy was sure she detected a startled look on Mary's face. Then the former waitress laughed heartily. "Oh, Miss Drew, isn't that funny you should have found that?"

"Then you knew lilacs are called 'blue pipes'?" Nancy asked. "And what in the world did the message mean?"

After a short pause, Mary answered, "I don't know. Someone asked me to write it."

"Who?"

"I don't remember his name. I wasn't there long, you know."

Nancy went through the list of names of the gardeners, but Mary still insisted she did not remember who had asked her to print the message.

"Another thing," said Nancy. "I phoned this house the other day and was told no Mary Mason who had worked at Lilac Inn was here."

Mary Mason flushed. "I don't know who answered the phone. Around here nobody calls me Mary. That's my business name. I'm Dotty Mae. My full name is Dorothy Mary."

"I see," said Nancy. "Sorry."

Mary stood up. "Hate to rush you, Miss Drew. But I'm er—expecting company."

She accompanied Nancy to the door. The young sleuth said good-by and went to her car. She started the engine, glancing surreptitiously at the Masons' cottage. Nancy plainly saw the window curtain move, as if someone were standing behind it, watching her.

As she drove away, Nancy reviewed the conversation. Mary Mason had seemed quite friendly, and sometimes a bit flighty. Nancy reflected that Mary's explanation of the "blue pipes" note sounded logical, but that the woman's whole story had been overly glib. She had, Nancy felt, not been entirely truthful.

"Why didn't she want to tell *me* who asked her to write the note about 'blue pipes'?" Nancy's hands gripped the wheel hard as a startling idea occurred to her. "She's shielding someone."

"Blue pipes" *was* being used as a signal—perhaps between persons at Lilac Inn and an outside accomplice. Were Mary Mason and a gardener two of them? And could Maud possibly be a third member of the group? Were they responsible for the diamond theft?

"They're all familiar with the place," Nancy

reasoned, "and might have learned of the secret closet."

If this were the case, she speculated, the three might have other assistants. "For instance," Nancy thought, "the woman who bumped into me in Benton, whoever put the diamond in my purse, and the person who placed the bomb in our cottage."

Nancy felt excitedly that her theory was worth following. She decided to return home and see if her father were there.

When Nancy arrived she was delighted to find Carson Drew at the desk in his study. The lawyer went over the whole case with his daughter, then shook his head in amazement. "This is a many-sided case you've tackled," he remarked. "I'm inclined to agree that the mysteries at Lilac Inn and your impersonator are linked together, and that 'blue pipes' *is* a signal of some kind."

Mr. Drew leaned forward in his chair. "Of course," he said, "Emily should report her entire story to the police. If Maud Potter does hold a threat over Mrs. Willoughby, she'll be dealt with by the law.

"Frankly I'm more alarmed about the spear throwing and time bomb than any other angle to the case, Nancy," Mr. Drew said somberly. "You and Helen are in constant danger."

Nancy said she realized this. "I'll be on my guard every minute," she promised. "And keep my eyes and ears open for any more 'blue pipe' messages."

The young detective went across the room to hug her father. "Dad, it's so helpful to talk everything over with you."

Mr. Drew looked at his daughter keenly. "There's something else on your mind. Want to tell me?"

He had observed a troubled expression come over Nancy's pretty features. Now she replied, "Yes. Dad, what's your impression of Sergeant John McBride?"

"I think he's a fine, intelligent young man," Mr. Drew said. "And seems to be quite taken with you," he teased.

Nancy's face remained serious. "I like him, too. But—well, Helen has a feeling he's at the inn for some other purpose than just helping Em and Dick."

Mr. Drew shook his head. "Nancy, don't worry. John may have his own reasons for being at Lilac Inn. But I firmly believe he's *not* mixed up in any jewel theft!"

With a smile Nancy said, "You're such a good judge of character. I knew you'd relieve my mind."

The lawyer then advised his daughter, despite Emily Willoughby's concern, to phone Chief Mc-Ginnis and tell him the whole story.

"He can use his own judgment on how to proceed. Also, he can dismiss the police guard at our home."

Nancy put in the call and gave the chief a detailed report, including the appearance of the stolen red truck in Dockville.

"I'll notify the authorities there at once," he said.

She inquired if there were police records of Dorothy Mary (Dotty Mae) Mason, Maud Potter, or any of the gardeners at Lilac Inn.

"I'll check." When the officer returned to the phone, he said, "No, Nancy. Nothing."

She promised to keep in touch and hung up. The girl's thoughts spun from subject to subject. Suddenly a daring plan popped into her head. "I'll try it!" Nancy decided.

Again she picked up the telephone. This time she dialed Lilac Inn. Emily answered.

"I think I'm making progress," Nancy told her friend. "I may not see you until tomorrow morning. Will you explain to everyone?"

"Of course." Emily then said happily that Dick had arrived. Her fiancé had learned from the explosives expert that the cottage fire definitely had been caused by a time bomb. The police were still working on the case.

Nancy said good-by, and mentally rehearsed her plan. "I've had sleuthing adventures before," she thought. "But this will be the first time I've impersonated a 'ghost'!"

CHAPTER XIII

The Guard's Mistake

WHEN Nancy confided to her father the idea of impersonating the ghostly woman in the lilac grove, Mr. Drew looked dubious.

"I think it's risky, Nancy. And also, how do you know any of the gang is going to see you?"

"I don't. I only hope so. But, Dad, if I'm convincing enough, someone may call me by her name, and I may learn to whom she was signaling, without raising suspicion."

Reluctantly Mr. Drew gave his consent. "If anything goes wrong, scream as loudly as you can."

"I will. But I intend to do a good acting job," Nancy assured her father.

Right after supper she went to the attic and opened a storage trunk. From it Nancy took out a white evening dress, long-sleeved and flowing. A further search disclosed a black wig she had once used at a costume party, and a transparent white scarf.

"Just the props I need," Nancy thought.

Returning to her room, Nancy tried on the hairpiece. To her satisfaction it completely hid her own hair. Next, she wired pocket-size flashlights to the cuff of each sleeve of the gown.

"These provide a glowing effect," she thought.

Nancy packed the wig and dress in her suitcase. Then she went downstairs and kissed her father and Hannah good-by.

"I wish you weren't going back to Lilac Inn," Hannah fretted.

"Now, Hannah," said Mr. Drew, "you know Nancy wouldn't give up any mystery until it's solved."

He then requested his daughter to telephone him the next morning. Nancy promised and left the house. She reached Benton at eight o'clock. Dusk was closing in, but it had to be considerably darker before Nancy could proceed to Lilac Inn.

She took a side road out of town. "Doris lives close to the inn," she recalled. "I'll drop in to see her." Presently she drove into a dirt lane leading to the Drakes' attractive white farmhouse.

She found Doris and her parents playing croquet on the front lawn. They greeted her cordially.

"About time you came to call," Doris scolded teasingly. "Nancy, any more news about your double?"

"Well, yes." Nancy smiled. "It's turned into quite a mystery, which I'm trying to solve."

"I understand. Detective at work," Doris guessed wisely.

Nancy then asked the Drakes if they knew a fisherman in the vicinity who wore his hair in a crew cut. They shook their heads.

"Does anyone own the dock between yours and the one at Lilac Inn?" Nancy questioned.

Mr. Drake replied that there was no house on the adjoining property. He understood the dock had been abandoned for years.

By the time Nancy took her leave and drew near the inn, it was dark. She decided to park in the apple orchard. As the girl detective got out of her car she felt raindrops. She took a plastic coat with attached hood from the trunk of her convertible and put it on. Then, carrying her suitcase, she dashed toward the inn.

When she reached it, Nancy circled the building cautiously, not wishing to be seen by anyone. The old inn was ablaze with lights. As Nancy approached the recreation room she heard dance music.

She crept up to the shrubbery and peered in. Helen and John were dancing, and Emily's partner was a young man of medium build with reddish-brown hair and a rather serious expression.

"That must be Dick," Nancy surmised. She observed that Maud, Mrs. Willoughby, and Mr.

Daly were talking in a far corner of the room.

"I'm glad they are having fun," Nancy thought, continuing around the inn. There was no sign near the building of the guard her father had obtained. No doubt he was down near the river. Nancy walked to the guest cottages, hoping that one might not be locked. Nancy tried the doors and finally came to one that opened.

"Brrrr!" she shivered, stepping into the chilly, damp room. Nancy's eyes quickly became accustomed to the gloom. The place had no furniture but a chair. "I'll have plenty of time to get ready. The ghost won't be out until the inn is dark. I may as well rest and go over my act," she thought, and sat down on the chair. "I only hope my masquerade will bring results."

The time crept by slowly, but finally Nancy saw by the luminous dial of her watch that it was eleven-thirty. She looked out the window. The rain had stopped and a few stars twinkled above.

All the lights in the inn were out. She noticed that John's cottage, too, was in darkness. "That's funny. He must have come back, but I haven't heard any footsteps since I've been here," Nancy mused. "Wonder where he is."

She opened her suitcase and lifted out the dress and wig. She put them on and took a small flashlight from her handbag.

Cautiously the masquerader made her way to the lilac grove, taking care not to stumble over roots or twigs. As she drew near it, Nancy thought she heard the distant put-put of a motorboat. But the sound soon faded away.

An owl hooted nearby. The darkness beneath the overhanging trees seemed forbidding. Suddenly Nancy felt panicky, but resolutely she put aside her fears. She clicked on the small flashlights attached to her sleeves and walked toward the spot where Helen had been struck. Dramatically, Nancy waved her arms back and forth.

"I wonder if someone will reply," she thought.

At the same moment she heard a noise in the underbrush. A small animal darted across her path, followed by the crunch of footsteps. Quickly extinguishing her lights, Nancy ducked behind a tall lilac.

The girl's heart pounded. A figure in glowing white moved slowly toward her hiding place. At this moment the moon came out from behind a cloud, illuminating the grove.

Nancy gasped. The other girl was in a long trailing gown. But Nancy felt as though she were looking into a mirror. The young woman's face seemed identical to Nancy's and she wore her titian-blond hair in exactly the same fashion Nancy usually did.

"My impersonator!" Nancy cried out involuntarily.

The strange woman stopped abruptly. She scanned the area with her eyes. Nancy came to a

"I only hope my masquerade will bring results"

sudden decision: she would meet her "twin" face to face!

Without hesitation Nancy clicked on her lights and darted from behind the bush. She confronted the other figure in white. The young woman gave a start of complete surprise upon seeing Nancy. Before either could say a word, heavy footsteps were heard approaching.

The strange girl turned and fled. The next instant Nancy's arm was seized by a man. "Let go of me!" she cried.

The man relaxed his grip and Nancy whirled around to face him. He was tall, husky, and wore slacks and a sports shirt.

"Who are you?" she asked.

"I'm a guard—Carl Bard."

"I'm Carson Drew's daughter, Nancy," she said quickly. "We must catch the young woman. She's an impostor and—"

She broke off. Carl Bard was staring at her in obvious disbelief. "I don't see anybody else, only you, miss. But Mr. Drew told me his daughter is blond."

In dismay, Nancy remembered the black wig she was wearing. "Oh—this is sort of a masquerade," she explained, snatching off the wig and hiding it inside her sleeve. "I'm visiting at Lilac Inn, and I know that my father suggested you come here."

"True. But I heard Miss Willoughby say Nancy

Drew wouldn't be returning tonight." The guard's tone was still suspicious. Again he gripped Nancy's arm. "You'd better come to the inn with me. We'll find out who you are."

Exasperated, Nancy cried out "You must believe me. There was another girl here! She escaped just before you saw me. She's a thief!"

The guard was adamant, and Nancy had no choice but to accompany him.

"My disguise certainly boomeranged," Nancy thought in disgust as she snapped off the flashlights in her sleeves.

When they reached the inn the guard rang the bell of the back door, which was closest. In a few minutes Emily and Maud appeared, both in robes and slippers.

"Mr. Bard! Is something wrong?" Emily asked, after flicking on the outside light.

"I found this young woman—" the guard began as he and Nancy stepped inside.

"Nancy Drew!" Emily exclaimed. "We didn't expect you until tomorrow!"

"And all dressed up, too. Been to a dance?" Maud asked curiously.

Nancy noticed that the social director wore full make-up. Had she really been in her room, or could Maud Potter have been the person Nancy's double was to meet in the grove? If so, Maud might have seen Nancy and returned to the inn before she was discovered!

Now Nancy flashed Emily a warning glance and answered, "Had an interesting date."

Emily caught on quickly. She turned to Carl Bard. "It's all right. This *is* Nancy Drew."

The guard nodded. "I'm convinced. But—"

Before he had a chance to say anything more, Nancy said with emphasis, "I'll explain everything *later*."

The man shrugged, said good night, and left.

"Did you have a good time this evening, Nancy?" asked Emily with a twinkle.

"I always do," Nancy replied airily, for Maud's benefit.

Just then a pleasant voice broke in, "Somebody arriving at this late hour?"

Dick Farnham came forward to join them. Emily smilingly introduced her fiancé to Nancy.

"I certainly appreciate all you've done to help us," Dick told Nancy. "It's a lucky thing you came to Lilac Inn."

"Now we'd all better get some rest," Emily said, and everyone agreed.

Nancy was first to reach the stairway. As she stepped up, her foot caught in the hem of her gown. She stumbled, and the black wig fell from her sleeve to the floor.

Maud glared at it. "Hm!" she said disdainfully. "Have you been up to some sleuthing trick?"

The secret of Nancy having masqueraded on the grounds was likely to be guessed by this busybody!

CHAPTER XIV

Earthquake Scare

"TIRED of being a blonde, Nancy?" Maud asked sarcastically. "Or are you the mysterious ghost of Lilac Inn?"

Emily, although at first surprised, sensed that Nancy had used the wig for a good reason. With a wink at Dick, she said, "Nonsense. I'll bet Nancy's date took her to a masquerade dance."

The young sleuth was grateful for Emily's quick thinking. Nancy waited for another outburst from Maud, but none came. Instead, the unpleasant woman said in a bored tone, "I think masquerades are so childish. Well, I'm going to bed." She said good night and went upstairs.

Nancy now turned to the engaged couple. "Are you both too tired to stay up a little longer?"

Dick grinned. "Not if I'm going to hear why one of Emily's pretty bridesmaids-to-be is masquerading as Cinderella. Tell me, Nancy, is it a new style to wear flashlights on your dress sleeves?"

"What!" Emily cried, and examined Nancy's sleeves. "Why, Nancy, what on earth *have* you been up to?"

"Can we talk some place where we won't be overheard?" Nancy requested. Dick led the way to his office.

Once inside, Nancy told of her sleuthing activities and experiences that day and night. "I'm glad you helped me along with that 'dance' story, Emily. Only Dad and the guard and you two know where I've been."

Dick spoke up earnestly, "You might be risking your life for us, Nancy. Lilac Inn isn't worth that."

Nancy set her jaw. "I must outwit my impersonator before she outwits me. And if I do, I'm positive I'll solve the mysteries of this place, too."

Dick nodded understandingly. He said Emily had told him of all the odd happenings at Lilac Inn.

"I also explained to Dick about my fear that Maud has some hold over Aunt Hazel," Emily said, adding that she hesitated to ask her aunt outright unless necessary.

"Of course," Nancy said. "Mrs. Willoughby is upset as it is."

Emily said grimly, "If I find out Maud is threatening my aunt, she'll regret it!"

The three young people started upstairs once

more. On the way, Nancy asked if Mary Mason and the gardeners had brought references when they came to Lilac Inn.

"Why, yes," Emily answered. "But at the time, Dick and I were so busy with work here, we didn't check them until later. They seemed all right."

The trio said good night, and Nancy entered her room. Helen was sleeping soundly, and did not awaken. It seemed to the young sleuth that her own eyes had just closed when she was awakened by Helen calling her name frantically.

"Nancy! Nancy! Wake up! There's an earthquake!"

"What?" Nancy sat up in bed. As she did the startled girl noticed that her bed was indeed shaking slightly.

"Quick!" Helen urged. "Let's get out of here before the ceilings fall down!"

As the girls ran to the hall, they met Dick, Emily, Mr. Daly, Mrs. Willoughby, and Maud. All cried out that they too had felt the vibrations, which now had ceased.

"This is very strange," Dick said. "This isn't earthquake territory."

On a hunch, Nancy suggested they telephone the Benton State Police and find out if the tremors were widespread. Dick made the call and with a puzzled expression reported that apparently the disturbance was confined to Lilac Inn.

Maud shrieked, "The building's falling apart! We'd better get out of here!"

"Go if you want to," Emily said sharply. "But the shaking has stopped and the building is still intact."

"I'll make an investigation," Dick offered. "There may be something wrong with the foundation." He suggested that Nancy and Mr. Daly accompany him to the cellar. "The rest of you wait here."

None of the three discovered anything out of the ordinary in the basement.

Nancy smiled in relief. "Instead of falling down, this building seems to be unusually sturdy."

Mr. Daly, however, was extremely nervous. "This has never happened before," he said. "Dick, I strongly advise you to give up the inn. It's—it's just not safe here any more."

Emily's fiancé shook his head, saying that he, like Nancy, was more determined than ever to solve the mysteries at Lilac Inn. The trio went back to the second floor and reassured the others.

"Are you all sure you never felt a similar vibration before?" Dick asked. "Shaking like that used to happen to our house when a very heavy truck went by."

"Maybe that's what happened this time," Helen said philosophically. "Let's go back to bed."

Nancy was not convinced by this explanation. Remembering the explosion and fire caused by the time bomb, she wondered if someone had planted an explosive underground to try to destroy or at least weaken Lilac Inn.

"Nancy," said Helen, when the girls were once more in bed, "why did you change your mind and come back to the inn tonight?"

When she heard about Nancy's masquerade in the lilac grove and its results, she praised her friend. "Next time, though, don't try such a risky thing alone," Helen scolded.

Nancy was almost asleep when a sudden thought struck her. Why had the "ghost" been titian-haired this time, instead of brunette?

When the girls went into the dining room the next morning, the other young people, Maud, and Mrs. Willoughby were already eating.

"Welcome back, Nancy," said John, grinning. "How's my beautiful sleuthing skin diver?"

"Ready to flip!" gibed Nancy.

Maud looked up from her grapefruit. "Will you go skin diving with a wig on?" she asked with an attempt to be facetious.

Nancy was slightly annoyed but gave no sign of this. She hoped Maud had not spread word around the inn of the wig episode.

Breakfast over, Nancy returned her car to the parking lot and then sought out Emily privately. She asked whether Maud had been gossiping about events of the previous evening. Emily said she was sure this was the case.

"Tell me, Emily," Nancy said, "how much do you know of Maud's background?"

"Very little. Only that Aunt Hazel met her about a year ago at a social gathering in River Heights. They became friendly. The next thing I heard was that Maud was going out West. Then, about a month ago, she showed up here. Aunt Hazel thought she would make a good social director, and Dick and I engaged her."

"Maud *can* be pleasant," Nancy commented, "and she does have musical talent. I really can't figure her out." To herself, Nancy conjectured on the possibility of Maud's using her position as a cover-up.

The young detective left the inn presently to do some sleuthing in the lilac grove. She met John part way there.

"I didn't want to mention it at breakfast, Nancy," he said, "but I'd like to see the exact site of your masquerade. Emily and Dick told me a little about it."

"I'll be glad to show you." Nancy led him to the lilac grove. She described vividly her encounter with her double. John listened intently.

"Nancy, you were in a dangerous spot. Maybe it's a lucky thing Carl Bard scared your impersonator away."

Nancy did not agree. "The sooner she is caught, the better. I must say, she does look much like me. I don't wonder you were fooled."

John laughed. "I think I wouldn't make the same mistake again. I much prefer the real Nancy."

Nancy blushed at his compliment. As the two looked about the lilac grove, Nancy saw a tiny object glinting in the sun. She picked it up. The object was of steel and shaped something like a can opener, except that there was a tiny wheel at the end.

"What's this?" she asked John.

He took the little device and stared at it. "I know where it belongs," he said. "I'll return it."

John put the object in his pocket, and Nancy had the feeling he had deliberately evaded her question.

"I wonder if there are any distinguishing footprints," he said, changing the subject.

Nancy frowned as she looked at the soft earth. There *was* a print—a peculiar one which she recognized—clearly outlined. It had been made by a skin diver's flipper. Nancy's mind flashed back to the night before, when she had left for the lilac grove. John's cottage had been dark. Maybe he had been sleeping. If not, where had he been?

"John," she said, looking the young man squarely in the eye, "were you skin diving last night?"

CHAPTER XV

The Underwater Rescue

JOHN MCBRIDE looked startled at Nancy's sudden query. "No, I wasn't skin diving," he said, returning the girl's direct look. "Why?"

Nancy pointed to the marks on the ground. "They're flipper prints," she said. "There must be more! The jeep tread and these prints have to start and end some place."

John knelt down and studied the prints. "From the size, I'd judge these were made by a man."

Nancy suddenly recalled the similar prints she had seen and the distant sound of a motorboat she heard as she had approached the grove the previous night. She told John of this. "Perhaps," she said, "whoever wore the flippers was to meet my impersonator and leave by boat."

"Or perhaps the diver was aboard but got out of the boat away from shore and swam underwater to avoid being detected," John guessed.

Nancy nodded and thought, "If this is the case,

it eliminates Maud Potter as a participant in the rendezvous."

Nancy's mind flitted over possible suspects. One of the gardeners? He could easily have skin-diving equipment without anyone knowing it.

As Nancy and John walked toward the river, following the flipper treads, she asked, "John, do you know what 'blue pipes' are?"

"Sure. Lilacs," he said matter-of-factly.

Nancy hesitated, then revealed her theory about the term being a code or a signal. "It could even mean Lilac Inn."

He raised his eyebrows in amazement. "Wow! Some shrewd deducing!" he exclaimed.

John stopped suddenly and grasped Nancy's arm. As the girl stared at him in surprise, he said excitedly, "Nancy! You've given me a terrific idea! I can't explain until—well, someday you'll understand."

Nancy's curiosity was piqued. She naturally did not ask John what he meant. But she was certain that he was tackling some secret problem. What was it?

By now the couple had reached the river. John pointed out three flipper prints in soft dirt patches along the bank.

Nancy scanned the area. "I'd like to have a look underwater here," she said. "John, would you like to make a skin-diving date?"

John grinned. "You couldn't keep me ashore."

The two returned to the inn. Nancy went first to the phone and called her father. Since she did not want to mention specific details in case someone was eavesdropping, she merely told him that "last night's meeting was most interesting."

"I understand," Mr. Drew said.

"Also, Dad, is it all right if I go skin diving? John will accompany me."

Mr. Drew gave his permission. "Perhaps you'll see some unusual fish," he added meaningfully.

"Could be, Dad. I'll let you know."

After Nancy had said good-by, she and John confided their plan and the reason for it to Helen, Emily, and Dick.

"All right," said Emily worriedly, "but watch out for spear throwers."

Soon Nancy and John, ready for skin diving, were back at the riverbank. They had decided to search underwater from the area of the flipper prints to the place Nancy had spotted the sharklike object.

They adjusted their face plates and tanks, and then they descended. Down—down they went, finally reaching the muddy bottom.

Their eyes darted here and there, observing schools of little fish; but nothing out of the ordinary came to sight. Nancy and John continued on, until they reached the place where Nancy had been before. They linked hands and walked cautiously along the river bottom.

Nancy pointed out the rocky overhang from which she had seen the shark shape projecting. John nodded.

To Nancy's disappointment, there was no sign of anything resembling the mysterious object. What had it been, she puzzled? A sunken boat that might have since drifted away?

Suddenly John stumbled and dropped Nancy's hand. Startled, she saw that his foot was wedged between two rocks obscured by weeds. He bent down and tugged, but to no avail.

At once Nancy went to his assistance. First, she pulled away the plant life surrounding the rocks. Then gently she tried to ease John's foot loose. It would not budge.

Nancy worked desperately to dislodge one of the rocks. Finally, with John's help, she succeeded in moving one of the stones. John's foot was free!

Exhausted, the couple rose to the surface and swam toward shore, gulping in fresh air. As soon as they sat down on the bank, John thanked Nancy for coming to his rescue. "You're a wonderful partner to have around, Nancy—sleuthing or skin diving," he said.

Nancy smiled. "Thanks, John. Let's have a look at your foot and see if it's injured."

John sighed. "Yes, Nurse."

They found that his foot was merely scraped. He and Nancy went underwater again to do some more sleuthing. But they uncovered nothing suspicious. Baffled, they swam back to their starting point and walked toward the inn.

On the way, Nancy saw Gil Gary trimming a hedge nearby. She and John went over to him.

"Do you happen to know anyone else around here who skin-dives, Gil?" Nancy asked.

The gardener did not look up, and continued his trimming. "Naw," he muttered. "River bottom's too muddy. It—"

He broke off. Nancy felt a surge of excitement. Why did Gil assume she was referring to the river? And did he know of its muddy condition from personal experience? Why had he not finished his answer?

"I suppose," she said, "some people prefer to travel by canoe." Nancy looked directly at the dock where one of the inn's canoes was tied up.

"S'pose so," Gil replied shortly.

John now stepped forward. "By the way, Gil, have you or Hank noticed any more tools missing lately?"

"Naw." The gardener shook his head.

John shrugged casually. "Just wondered, because Miss Drew and I came across a funny gadget this morning. Sort of like a can opener. Sound familiar?"

"No!" the gardener snapped. He flung his shears to the ground. "I'm goin' for lunch," he said, and retreated hastily.

Nancy and John exchanged triumphant glances.

"He's nervous about something, all right," John said.

"He certainly doesn't act like an innocent person," Nancy reasoned.

There was just time before luncheon for Nancy and John to report in private to their three young friends.

When Dick heard of the gardener's reaction to Nancy's queries, he frowned. "Maybe I should have a talk with him myself," he said.

Nancy advised against this action for the present. "If Gil is connected with the diamond theft, we may learn through him who else is involved," she pointed out. "And, perhaps, the identity of my double."

"You mean, all the culprits might be trapped at once?" Helen asked, and Nancy nodded.

As Nancy sat down at the table with the others, Jean came over. "Thanks again for the ride, Miss Drew," she said in her shy way. "It was real helpful."

At this moment Maud Potter entered the room. Jean quickly bent over and whispered to Nancy, "Don't forget! Watch out for that trouble-maker."

Nancy did not know what to think. She disliked Maud, but felt it was unfair to accept Jean's claim without proof. "Don't trust an informer too far," her father had once said.

The social director took her place. Looking at

Emily, she announced, "Your aunt has a splitting headache and won't be down."

"Oh, poor dear." Emily jumped up. "I'll go see—"

"I wouldn't disturb her," Maud interrupted officiously. "She'll feel better after some rest."

Emily's eyes blazed. "If I want to see my aunt, Maud, I shall. I'm sick and tired of your meddling. Dick and I are paying you to be social director— and—and nothing else!"

There was dead silence at the girl's outburst. Then Maud gasped. "Well! That's all the thanks I get."

"Thanks for what!" Emily stormed. "Keeping Aunt Hazel under your thumb and being unpleasant to my guests?"

By now everyone in the dining room—waitresses and patrons—were staring in Emily's direction. Dick tried to intervene. "Em, calm down," he begged. "We'll discuss it later."

But Emily, overwrought, paid no attention. "I don't care. I'll give up Lilac Inn rather than see Aunt Hazel unhappy. I wouldn't be surprised, Maud Potter, if you're responsible for the awful things that have happened here!"

An almost bewildered look came over Maud's flushed face. She started to protest, "I most certainly did not—"

Emily did not allow her to finish. "Furthermore," the girl went on, "I'm going to notify the police about all my suspicions regarding the diamonds immediately."

At this point Nancy happened to notice that Jean Holmes was taking in the scene with avid interest. For a fleeting moment the sleuth detected a hard, calculating look replacing Jean's usually shy expression. But the next moment the waitress picked up a tray and went toward the kitchen.

In the meantime, Maud had also risen. "By all means call the police. It's about time they learn the truth," she said, with a scornful glance at Nancy. Declaring she had lost her appetite, the woman left the room.

Pale and trembling, Emily sat down. "I'm sorry," she said weakly. "I just couldn't take Maud's arrogance another minute."

"I don't blame you," Helen spoke up sympathetically, then whispered, "At least Maud didn't act as if she were mixed up with the theft of the diamonds."

"That's right," Dick conceded. "But where do we go from here? Unless this mystery's cleared up, we may not be able to open the inn in July. Also," he added glumly, "Emily and I might have to postpone our wedding."

"Oh, no!" Emily wailed.

Dick said he could foresee no other course of

action. His funds were low, and if he and Emily were to make a success of the resort, the necessary outdoor work must be completed. A pool and tennis courts, yet to be built, had been especially featured in his publicity campaign.

"I've already mailed out thousands of brochures," he said.

"Yes, and we're booked almost solid for summer reservations," Emily said unhappily. "Oh, Nancy, what shall we do? I hate to give up hope of getting my diamonds back."

Nancy replied firmly, *"I'm* not giving up. If you agree, Emily and Dick, there are a few more angles of this case I want to investigate. And if you don't mind, I'd like to tell Lieutenant Brice the whole story."

The engaged couple readily consented. "Nothing matters now except finding out the truth," Emily said.

After lunch Nancy drove to Benton. For privacy, she telephoned the State Police officer from a booth in the drugstore there. When Nancy had finished her account, he assured her he would do all he could to turn up possible new leads to Nancy's impersonator. Then Nancy called Chief McGinnis. The typed envelope, he said, had brought no results.

"I'll confer with Lieutenant Brice about happenings at Lilac Inn. By the way, no luck yet in finding the stolen truck."

Nancy's next call was to her father. Mr. Drew confessed alarm upon hearing the details of his daughter's meeting with her double. "No telling what she and her accomplices may be up to," he warned. "But whatever you do, Nancy, don't overstep anyone's legal rights."

"I'll remember."

By the time Nancy returned to the inn, it was late afternoon. The sky had filled with black clouds, and the air was close and oppressive. "There's going to be a thunderstorm," Nancy thought as she entered the lobby.

No one was in sight. But just then Mr. Daly came from his office. He said that nothing had been found to account for the quakelike vibrations.

"I'm afraid, Mr. Daly," Nancy said, "that the cause is man-made. How, I don't know yet."

The former owner of the inn was shocked. "To think this fine building must endure such treatment!" He told Nancy that the inn had been built in 1760 by an English family, and had catered to both stagecoach and river travelers. The inn had passed from one generation of the original family to the next. "Some people said that Lilac Inn was a refuge for slaves who had escaped from the South."

"Maybe that's why the secret room was built," Nancy remarked. "Who owned the inn previous to you?" she asked.

"A Spaniard named Ron Carioca who'd lived in the West Indies. It was he who planted the beautiful lilac tree—for good luck—outside the front entrance."

Just then Mr. Daly's phone rang, and he excused himself to answer it. Nancy walked on into the dining room and looked out the bay window. The sky was getting darker each minute.

"Oh, hello, Miss Drew." The voice was Jean Holmes'. She carried a large vase filled with yellow iris and reddish-purple lilacs, which she set on the window sill.

"You seem to like flowers, Jean," Nancy observed. "That's a pretty combination: iris and 'blue pipes.' "

" 'Blue pipes'?" Jean echoed. "What made you use that expression?"

"It's different," Nancy said nonchalantly.

Did the waitress seem suddenly ill at ease, or was it Nancy's imagination? Before the young sleuth could decide, there was a loud clap of thunder, followed by the banging of several shutters. As Jean and Mr. Daly hurried to shut the dining-room windows, Nancy saw John and Dick dash across the side lawn toward the inn.

Rain came pouring down in silvery sheets. There was another resounding thunderclap, then a vivid flash of lightning. A splintering, crashing sound followed.

"Oh!" Jean shrieked. "The inn's been struck!"

CHAPTER XVI

A Letter

THE crash had come from the front of the inn. Everyone raced through the lobby to peer outside.

"Oh!" Nancy cried. "The historic lilac tree is down."

The lovely "tree of good fortune" had fallen onto the lawn, splintered and charred.

"More bad luck!" Emily said mournfully.

Suddenly Maud burst out, "This is the last straw! I'm fed up with a place full of thieves, weird noises, bombs, a trembling building— I quit."

She turned a scathing look on Mrs. Willoughby. "You got me into this. Thanks for nothing! I've found a better job on my own!"

Emily's face was expressionless as Maud snapped open her purse and fumbled through its contents. She drew out a letter and flourished it.

"This is an offer of a position I received today

from the Hotel Claymore in River Heights. I've already accepted it," Maud stated. "Emily, I didn't go to the employment agency just to find you a waitress, but to find a *decent* job for myself. But I asked the manager not to say I had been there."

With dignity Emily said, "Maud, Dick will write a check for whatever salary we owe you."

With a triumphant air Maud marched upstairs. Emily looked around anxiously. The waitresses and cooks had gathered in a corner of the hall. Obviously they had not missed a word of what had been said.

Nancy sensed what her friend was thinking: that the employees were probably suspicious about the fire. Now that Maud had mentioned the bomb, all of them might become alarmed enough to give notice. Prospects for Lilac Inn's success would indeed be dim.

"I must help Em and Dick before it's too late," Nancy told herself determinedly.

As the rain abated and the sky began to brighten, the men went outside to examine the fallen lilac. Nancy now turned to Mrs. Willoughby, who seemed almost in a daze. "Perhaps you'd better sit down and rest," she said kindly.

Emily's aunt gave a great sigh. "I will. Please come with me to Emily's office," she asked the three girls.

When they were seated, Emily said, "Aunt Hazel, *was* Maud Potter threatening you in some way?"

"I'm afraid so," Mrs. Willoughby replied wearily. "Actually I believe she wouldn't have carried it out. But I couldn't be sure—"

To the girls' dismay, the woman broke down and sobbed. Nancy patted her shoulder. "Won't you tell us about it?"

Regaining composure, Mrs. Willoughby nodded. "I feel terrible. When I brought Maud here, I thought I was helping Emily and Dick. But it's turned out just the opposite.

"Anyhow," she went on, "I met Maud a year ago at a party in River Heights. We became friendly—attended the theater and so forth. Maud seemed very pleasant and good company at the time. And I also felt sorry for her."

"Sorry?" Helen echoed.

Mrs. Willoughby explained that Maud's husband had died several years before, leaving her penniless. Since then, she had worked at various resorts, but not very long at any one.

"When Maud heard about Lilac Inn, she persuaded me that, with her experience, she'd be ideal as social director. But soon after her arrival here, she asked me to lend her a large sum of money—claimed to have a lot of unpaid bills which her salary wouldn't cover. Maud became angry when I refused, but she continued her demands for money."

Emily interrupted, "Aunt Hazel, why didn't you tell us she was bothering you? Dick would have asked her to leave."

"Maud insinuated that if I tried to force her to leave, she would say that—that *I* had stolen your diamonds, Emily, by getting them from the bank weeks ago, and substituting the fake stones!"

"How dreadful!" Nancy cried out, and Emily added fiercely, "That awful woman! But, Aunt Hazel, we never would have believed her."

"I know," Mrs. Willoughby said ruefully. "But with so many strange things happening, I guess I wasn't thinking logically."

Nancy had one more question to clear up regarding Maud Potter. She decided to mention Jean Holmes' warning about the woman.

"Did any of you notice Maud going into our cottage the day of the fire?" Nancy asked. "Or our room here?"

No one had. Furthermore, Mrs. Willoughby added, "I believe Jean must have been mistaken. When Maud wasn't with us, she stayed in her room typing. She probably was writing letters of application."

Presently Nancy excused herself, saying she wanted to take a walk and do some thinking. Once outside, she took a trail toward the river. Drops of rain still sparkled on the foliage.

Nancy's thoughts reverted to Jean's story about Maud. "It sounds as though the waitress might not have been telling the truth. But why would she want to incriminate Maud? And why did Jean appear so uneasy when I mentioned 'blue pipes'?"

The young sleuth suddenly roused from her concentration on the puzzle and became aware of an interesting, gnarled apple tree along the riverbank. Just then she noticed an envelope stuck in a crotch of the tree.

Nancy picked up the damp envelope, wondering if it had blown there during the storm or been placed in the crotch, perhaps for someone to find. There was no stamp or address on the envelope, only a name—Miss Lillie Merriwcather.

Suddenly Nancy's eye was caught by the fact that in the typed name the letter *a* was very faint. This, as well as the rest of the typing, reminded Nancy suddenly of the envelope found with her charge plate.

"I wonder if they were done on the same machine!" she thought excitedly.

The flap of the envelope had become unsealed from dampness and the girl slid the letter out easily. A pink lilac spray adorned the top left corner of the stationery. A message below it, all typed, read:

Dear Lillie:

I hope we can get together soon. I've been busy lining up an important job. Give my best to

your dad. Tell him I have a beautiful blue pipe
for him. Hope to see you soon.

Hastily, but with love,

Gay

Nancy's heart was thumping with excitement.
Lilacs—"blue pipes"—two envelopes bearing
the same type—was someone named *Gay* her impersonator?

"The name Lillie Merriweather sounds
vaguely familiar," the girl detective thought.

Hastily she slid the letter back into the envelope and put it in the tree. She would alert the
police to watch for anyone returning to look for
the letter.

As Nancy hurried back to the inn, she recalled
Mrs. Willoughby saying that Maud Potter had
been typing. By some chance was the director still
a possible suspect in the mystery? Was she the person who had typed the envelope containing
Nancy's charge plate?

"I'll check," Nancy determined. She went upstairs and knocked on Maud's bedroom door. It
was flung open by the director.

"Yes?" she snapped.

"May I come in?" Nancy asked.

Grudgingly, Maud allowed Nancy to enter and
the detective saw that a suitcase was nearly packed.
On a desk stood Maud's typewriter, with a blank
piece of paper in the roller.

"Well, Nancy, what do *you* want?" Maud asked.

Watching the woman closely, Nancy queried, "Have you heard from Gay or Lillie lately?"

"What?" Maud appeared flabbergasted. "I don't know any Gay or Lillie. Now stop quizzing me as if I had done something criminal."

"I suppose," Nancy said icily, "that practically blackmailing Mrs. Willoughby isn't?"

To her surprise, Maud burst into tears. Between sobs she told Nancy that she had never intended to carry out her threat. "I don't know why I did it. Hazel has been very good to me. I guess I've just been upset and worried about money ever since my husband's death."

Nancy could not help feeling a little sorry for the woman. Nevertheless, she asked, "Do you know anything about the time bomb that was set off in my cottage?"

"No!" Maud looked shocked. Nancy was sure she was telling the truth. "I've been jealous of you, Nancy," she admitted, "but I'd never do anyone physical harm."

As Maud dried her eyes, Nancy walked toward the desk. Nonchalantly she typed out her name on the typewriter. *N-a-n-c-y*. All the letters were clearly defined. The suspicious envelopes had definitely not been typed on this machine.

She turned to Maud, wished her good luck in her new position, and left. Then Nancy went downstairs and told Helen, Dick, and the Willoughbys about the letter and her interview with

Maud. "I'm convinced that Maud won't cause any more trouble," she stated. "And now, if you'll keep everyone out of earshot of the phone, I'll call the State Police and suggest they watch for Gay."

Nancy had just finished her conversation when Maud Potter came downstairs. She looked ashamed, and said she would not accept the check Dick offered her. She asked him to use the money for work on the resort. A few minutes later the ex-director left in a taxi.

Suddenly everyone was startled by Mr. Daly rushing frantically from his office.

"Gracious! What's the matter?" Mrs. Willoughby asked him.

"My blue pipe's missing! Has anyone seen it?"

"Do you mean the one you were carving from lilac wood?" Nancy asked.

Mr. Daly nodded, saying he had just completed work on the pipe a few hours ago. He had searched everywhere for it. Although the pipe was of no great value, he had promised it to a friend. No one present had seen the hand-carved piece.

"Why would anyone take it?" Helen puzzled.

At that moment Nancy recalled the wording of Gay's letter. "Tell him I have a beautiful blue pipe for him." Could Gay possibly have referred to Mr. Daly's pipe, and she, or some accomplice, have stolen it for Lillie's Dad? If so, Gay was certainly familiar with Lilac Inn and its occupants.

At that moment Nancy glanced into the dining

room. Jean Holmes was setting tables for supper. Suddenly Nancy had a vivid recollection of the shy waitress staring at Mr. Daly's pipe while he had been showing it to Nancy. Could Jean have stolen it for Gay? But for what reason?

Saying nothing of her speculations, Nancy asked her friends if the name Lillie Merriweather meant anything to them.

"There's an actress named Lillie Merriweather," Helen spoke up. "She plays bit roles on Broadway. I think now she has parts mostly in stock theaters throughout the country."

"That's right," said Mr. Daly. "In fact, I read that she's with a stock company in Bridgeton, about seventy-five miles from here."

"Helen, let's drive to Bridgeton tomorrow!" Nancy proposed excitedly. "I have a hunch Lillie Merriweather can tell us something about the mystery at Lilac Inn!"

CHAPTER XVII

The Net Tightens

HELEN eagerly agreed to go with Nancy to call on Lillie Merriweather, the actress. "It would be fun even if there weren't a mystery," she said.

A little later Lieutenant Brice arrived at the inn with another trooper. In Dick's office Nancy told him about Gay's letter and the spot near which she had found it.

"We'll keep watch," the officer promised. He took the other trooper aside and whispered instructions. The man nodded and left.

Lieutenant Brice then told Nancy and her friends that no clues had been discovered to the person who had placed the time bomb.

"There was an unusual silencer on it, however," he said. "That's why you didn't hear the ticking, Nancy, until a short time before the bomb was due to explode."

The officer also said that besides the red panel truck, several other cars in the area had been stolen. "Some of the vehicles have been recovered, but there's still no sign of the red truck. We'll keep looking," the lieutenant promised as he left.

Sunday morning Nancy and Helen were up early for church and their trip to Bridgeton. After breakfast the girls went to the parking lot. To their astonishment, Nancy's convertible was not there!

"Good night!" Nancy exclaimed. Rapidly she searched her handbag for the key. It was not there. "I must have left the key in the ignition!" she chided herself.

Helen groaned. "Your car probably was stolen by one of those thieves!"

Just then, John McBride drove into the lot in his jeep. "Hi!" he greeted the girls. "Why so glum?"

When Nancy told about her missing car, John suggested that he and the girls go off in his jeep and search the grounds before reporting the loss.

"Your car may only have been hidden by a prankster," he suggested. "This is the day for car trouble," he added. "I just fixed a flat tire."

Twenty minutes later the group spotted Nancy's convertible near a cornfield across the lane from the orchard. They examined the vehicle, and found it intact. The key was in the lock.

"Whoever took it had a short trip," John commented.

Nancy wondered whether the unknown driver had only played a prank. If so, why? To discourage her from going to Bridgeton? Or had the person planned to steal the car but been scared off?

The girls stepped into the convertible and told John their destination. "Lots of luck," he said.

The drive to Bridgeton took about an hour and a half. Nancy and Helen arrived in time to attend services in the quaint, white, eighteenth-century church. Then they had lunch at a tearoom.

"Where do we look for Miss Merriweather?" asked Helen as they paid their check. "The theater's closed today."

Nancy asked the tearoom manager where the summer stock people were living.

"At the Montrose Hotel, two blocks down."

Ten minutes later the girls walked into the small hotel. They learned from the desk clerk that the actress and her father had Suite 303.

As Nancy and Helen rode up in the elevator, they reviewed a plan they had worked out earlier. To avoid rousing suspicion, Nancy would pretend to be an actress named Dru Gruen. She would further pretend that she knew Gay but had lost contact. Helen was to pose as a dancer.

As the young sleuth knocked on the door of Suite 303, she was filled with anticipation. Would the visit yield the answer to the mystery, or would it prove to be only a false lead?

The door was opened by a tall, slim young woman, with silver-blond hair. She wore a becoming dress of jade-green silk.

"Yes?" she asked in a throaty voice.

Nancy smiled. "Miss Merriweather? I'm Dru Gruen, an actress, and this is my friend Helga Marsh, a dancer. I understand you know Gay. We're trying to locate her."

The actress looked startled. "Gay Moreau?"

"Yes," Nancy replied without hesitation.

Miss Merriweather invited her callers into an attractive living room. A fine-looking elderly man arose from a chair as they entered.

"Papa," said the actress, "these young ladies are theater people—Miss Gruen and Miss Marsh. They're looking for Gay."

Mr. Merriweather, too, appeared startled. "We haven't seen Gay in quite some time," he said. "May I ask why you're trying to find her?"

"We thought we'd like to have a little reunion," Nancy explained. "We haven't seen Gay recently, and don't know her present address."

"We don't know where she's living, either," Lillie put in. "I haven't heard from Gay since the last time I saw her."

"When was that?" Nancy asked.

"Shortly after she was released from prison."

Nancy and Helen were amazed to hear this. But they managed to conceal it.

"I imagine," Nancy said carefully, "that Gay's been having a hard time."

Lillie and her father agreed. "Very sad." Mr. Merriweather sighed. "Gay had talent. But a five-year sentence for check forgery doesn't help one's career."

"I can't understand why she did it," Nancy said.

"Probably because Gay was poor most of her life," Lillie reminisced. "Once success came her way, she spent all her earnings on luxuries. But Gay couldn't stop buying expensive things. I guess she figured forgery was the easiest way to get more money."

Mr. Merriweather frowned. "What bothered me was that Gay swore revenge on the person who was instrumental in having her sent to prison."

"The one whose signature she forged?" Helen asked.

"She didn't mention the name," replied Lillie's father.

"How old is Gay now?" Nancy inquired.

"About twenty-seven," Lillie answered.

"I wonder," Nancy pursued, "if she still likes 'blue pipes'?"

"Oh! Gay must've told you that means lilacs!" Lillie exclaimed. "She certainly was crazy about them—even wore lilac colors."

"Say!" Mr. Merriweather exclaimed. "I wonder

if Gay sent me the pipe made of lilac wood I received yesterday. There was no return address on the package, and the postmark was blurred—must've gotten wet."

When he showed the pipe to Nancy, she could scarcely hide her excitement. The pipe looked exactly like Mr. Daly's! But she asked Lillie in an offhand way if Gay had ever spoken of Lilac Inn.

"Why, yes," the actress replied. "If you mean the old place in Benton that Gay said she visited as a child, when the inn was owned by a relative of hers—someone who'd lived in the West Indies."

"He was a Spaniard, I believe," Nancy put in, "named Ron Carioca."

"That sounds right," Lillie said.

Mr. Merriweather spoke up, "You might find Gay in Benton. Maybe she went back for old times' sake."

"A good idea. We'll look there," Helen said.

Nancy sighed. "I suppose she's changed quite a bit since—her imprisonment."

Lillie shook her head. "Surprisingly, no. I'll show you." The actress went to a table and picked up a scrapbook of clippings. She thumbed through the pages and pointed out a recent magazine picture of an attractive model with golden hair. "This is Gay. Looks just like her."

The young sleuth studied the picture. It struck her there was something familiar about Gay's eyes.

The two girls thanked the Merriweathers and left. They got into the car and headed for Benton. Elatedly, Nancy and Helen discussed everything they had learned—Gay's last name, the fact that she had been in prison, and her childhood association with Lilac Inn.

"Do you think she *is* your double, Nancy?" asked Helen. "There's a resemblance. Besides, being an actress, Gay knows how to use make-up skillfully."

"Yes. Also, the color of her hair is similar to mine," Nancy added.

"But," said Helen, "I can't understand why Gay decided to impersonate you in the first place."

"I'm inclined to think it had nothing to do with the mystery of Lilac Inn in the beginning," Nancy replied. "She wanted clothes and jewelry, so took my charge plate. But later she decided to use the disguise to keep John and me from our skin-diving trip."

"You mean Gay was at the inn?"

"Yes. Under an assumed name, of course."

Helen grinned at the young sleuth. "And next you're going to tell me who she was. Well, one person she *couldn't* have been was Mary Mason. You saw her in Dockville, and said she's heavier and older than you."

Nancy pursed her lips. "I never checked the description of *that* Mary Mason with Emily. She may *not* have been the Mary who worked at the inn, but was in league with her, and was asked to pose as Mary Mason, waitress."

Helen was amazed. "Nancy, you're a whiz. Gay and Mary probably are the same person."

"That's what I suspect, Helen. First, we'll check with Emily."

When the girls reached the inn, they questioned Emily. "Now that I think of it, Nancy," Emily said, "Mary Mason *was* about your height and weight, and her coloring's like yours."

"That settles it," said the young sleuth. "I'm going to talk to Chief McGinnis immediately." With her friends covering the extension phones, Nancy told him of her suspicions.

"You've certainly made great progress, Nancy," he praised her. "I'll ask the Dockville police to get a line on the Mary Mason you talked to there."

"Thank you," said Nancy, then she called her father. Hannah said that Mr. Drew had gone out to dinner with a client, so Nancy asked the housekeeper to give him a message.

"Of course. Have you solved the mystery?" Hannah inquired hopefully.

Nancy said not yet, but to tell her father that she had an important clue to her impersonator. "Ask him to call me at the inn, please."

Hannah promised to do so, and said that she hoped to hear the whole story soon. At suppertime John was not present at the table. Helen asked nonchalantly where he was.

"John said he had an errand to do," Dick replied.

When the meal was over, Nancy encountered Jean Holmes in the center hall. "If anyone should phone me, will you please call me," she requested. "I'm going outside for a walk."

"I'll be glad to, Miss Drew," said the waitress.

Actually Nancy wanted to find Carl Bard and ask the guard if he had seen anything suspicious or obtained any clue to her double. She met him coming toward the inn to supper.

"No, I haven't," he replied to her questions. "It's been very quiet here."

Nancy thanked him and walked off. She strolled through the grounds, thinking over the day's events. Who had used her car? Had John any idea as to the driver's identity? Was it the person responsible for the flipper tracks John had examined several days ago in the orchard?

Nancy continued toward the water reflectively, but did look back, wondering if by chance anyone might be following her. Suddenly she saw Jean Holmes emerge from the kitchen door of the inn. No one else was in sight.

"She's probably looking for me," Nancy thought. "Chief McGinnis or Dad must have phoned."

Nancy expected Jean to call out her name, but she did not do so. The young sleuth was about to hail the girl when she noticed that Jean was carrying a small suitcase. She glanced furtively from left to right, then headed for the river. Some instinct caused Nancy to duck behind a large oak. Jean reached the water and turned right. Nancy stealthily followed the waitress.

The other girl walked on quickly until she reached the lilac grove. Then she slipped through an opening in the bushes.

Curious, Nancy decided to keep shadowing the waitress. The trail led Nancy upstream along the river for about half a mile. Presently Jean approached a dilapidated building. She entered the partially open, sagging front door.

As Nancy crept forward, she looked about her constantly. Suddenly she stifled a scream. A grotesque shape was emerging from the river!

The apparition had stubby back fins and a bulging glassed-in prow. It was about fifteen feet long and painted a somber blue.

Then recognition struck Nancy full force. "That's the 'shark' I saw underwater—a miniature submarine!"

Fascinated, she watched the craft glide into a cove adjacent to the shed. A moment later a man's hand lifted back the glassed-in section and a figure in skin-diving gear stepped to the ground.

Before Nancy could decide what to do, she was grabbed from behind and a rough hand was clapped over her mouth!

CHAPTER XVIII

A Submarine Prisoner

NANCY struggled but could not free herself or see her captor as she was pushed toward the shack. A cloth had been tied over her mouth. Once inside the dilapidated building, she blinked in astonished disbelief.

Jean Holmes stood peering into what looked like a cellar! Gil Gary, the gardener, was holding open a trap door to the opening!

Jean and Gil stared at Nancy and her captor. "Well, Nancy Drew, the detective!" Jean's voice was no longer shy, but strident. "Where did you find *her*, Frank?"

"Spying, was she?" Gil added.

"She sure was," said the man called Frank. The young detective observed that he was about fifty years old, and of medium build. His hair was cropped close. Suddenly Nancy realized that he must be the boatman with a crew cut whom Helen had seen and also the fisherman on the

"Nancy Drew won't get a chance to reveal our scheme!"

river she herself had questioned. She recognized his nasal voice.

But Jean! Nancy was astounded. What was this trio up to? Obviously something underhanded. Was Gay, alias Mary Mason, in league with them? And how did the miniature submarine fit into their scheme?

Frank maintained a tight grip on Nancy's arm. "Guess you won't go skin diving for a while." He gave a harsh laugh.

"You bet," Jean spoke up, her eyes gleaming coldly. Nancy noticed the girl no longer wore glasses. "We'll see to that. Nancy Drew won't ever get a chance to reveal our scheme!"

Gil nodded. "We've got to clear out pronto and take her with us. The shipment's aboard the boat. Everything's cleaned out of here."

The three accomplices held a whispered consultation. Before Nancy had time for further analysis, Gil looked at his watch.

"We've got to step on it. Simon will be worried."

"See you there," Jean said to Nancy slyly. "Try to figure this one out, Miss Private Eye!"

At these words, Frank gave Nancy a shove and dragged her to the river. The man in skin-diving gear was waiting. Nancy struggled to get away, but to no avail.

To her horror, the skin diver forced her into the back seat of the miniature submarine and tied her securely. She had a glimpse of Frank, Gil, and Jean boarding a motorboat hidden in a nearby cove. Then the skin diver shut the transparent hatch and the sub began to descend.

"How am I ever going to escape?" A wave of terror swept over the young sleuth. As the submarine plunged downward, Nancy told herself sternly, "I must keep cool!"

She noticed that the skin diver remained in front with another man, who was piloting the craft. "They're two more members of the gang," Nancy thought. "I wonder who Simon is? And what kind of shipment is on the boat Gil mentioned? Are we heading there now?"

The navigator was steering forward, using a simple control stick and automatic pedals. He and the frogman kept their backs turned to Nancy. Were these men enemy agents, or smugglers? Perhaps Emily's diamonds were part of the mysterious shipment!

Nancy thought about the rocky overhang under which the shark-nosed sub had been hidden. "I suppose Frank was the lookout," she conjectured. "And Gil probably went to meet him in a canoe from the inn."

She concluded that the skin diver had probably thrown the spear at her. "Either to get rid of me for good, or scare me away. And it was probably this sub that caused Helen and me to capsize in the canoe."

It occurred to Nancy that even if she learned the answers to all her questions, it might do her no good. Escape seemed impossible. She realized that none of her friends, her father, or the police would have the slightest idea where she was.

Then a faint hope came to her. Carl Bard had seen her leave the inn! "If only they think to search the river," Nancy thought worriedly.

Trying to forget her fears, the young sleuth concentrated on the two scheming waitresses: Mary, doubtless a disguise of Gay Moreau, and Jean Holmes who—

"It's fantastic—but—if Gay can impersonate me, and pose as Mary, why couldn't she be Jean Holmes?"

Nancy was sure the actress could easily play any role—plus being Gay herself! Gay, beautiful but avaricious; easygoing, flighty Mary, and shy, plain Jean.

Gay, familiar with the inn, had disguised herself as Mary. She could have been the "ghost," sometimes as a titian blonde, at others wearing a dark wig. As part of the scare operation, she had left, using the excuse of the place being haunted. Then she had come back in another disguise—as Jean Holmes.

Gay, as Mary, could easily have overheard Mrs. Willoughby describing Emily's twenty diamonds, and also telling Maud the planned date of presentation. Then Mary bought the substitutes. She had slipped into the hidden closet without being seen and committed the theft.

The speculation brought Nancy back to the present. Had Frank and the men on the sub helped with the diamond robbery? Was the cellar in the river shack being used to hide stolen goods to be taken away later in the sub? Would the answer to these questions explain the other mysterious events, including the time bomb and the vibrations at the inn, all done to scare people away from the place?

It seemed to the young sleuth that ages had gone by since her capture. But now the sub slowly ascended to the surface. Nancy heard the navigator say that something was wrong with the mechanism. As he steered toward a small cabin cruiser a few hundred feet away, Nancy saw that they were on an isolated section of the Muskoka River.

The sub stopped alongside the cruiser and the pilot opened the hatch. He untied Nancy from the seat and helped her mount a small ladder to the deck of the cruiser.

Awaiting them were Jean Holmes, Gil Gary, and Frank! Jean laughed triumphantly. "Well, have a nice trip?" she taunted Nancy.

Unable to speak, and guarded closely by Gil and Frank, holding flashlights, Nancy gave her a disgusted look. She scanned the river for other nearby craft. There were none. If only a River Police Patrol boat would come by! But none did,

Meanwhile, the skin diver and pilot had hitched the miniature submarine to the stern of the cruiser. As the diver took off his face mask, Nancy saw that he was dark, wiry, and had an impassive expression. Jean gestured toward the pilot, a stocky man of about thirty.

"This is my brother-in-law Bud," she smirked, as Gil tied Nancy's arms behind her back, then bound her legs together with a stout rope. "I couldn't introduce you when you visited my sister in Dockville. She did a good job of being Mary Mason, eh, Nancy?"

Nancy's theory about two Mary Masons was correct! Also, it was now apparent that Gay Moreau had assumed her brother-in-law's last name for her first Lilac Inn disguise.

The next moment Nancy was thrust violently forward through the door of a small cabin. She fell to the floor, and the door was slammed behind her. Simultaneously, the cruiser's engine churned and the boat began moving. Despair engulfed Nancy.

Meanwhile, back in River Heights, Chief McGinnis had just received a phone call from the Dockville chief. He reported that the house Nancy had visited was empty. Neighbors had said that the three occupants, a husband and wife and a woman relative had rented the house. They had been quiet, and kept to themselves.

One woman neighbor had mentioned, however, that occasionally she heard hammering and drilling noises coming from the basement of the house. The police sergeant had checked and discovered some electronic equipment in the cellar, along with several books on navigation and skin diving.

"But we found a real prize in the garage," the sergeant added. "The stolen truck that almost ran into Miss Drew! We're keeping a stake-out on the house."

Chief McGinnis had just hung up when a call came in from Carson Drew. "Chief," the lawyer said tersely, "have you heard from Nancy?"

"Not since this afternoon. Why?"

The lawyer explained that he had just returned home, and telephoned the inn. He had learned from Miss Willoughby that Nancy had been missing for several hours. "Everyone, including the State Police, are out looking for her. Nancy's convertible is still in the parking lot. Her canoe and diving equipment are still there.

"I don't like this at all," Carson Drew went on gravely. "I understand my daughter called you after talking with some actress who gave her a clue to the person who's been posing as Nancy."

"Yes, Nancy thinks her impersonator is an actress with a prison record. Her name is Gay Moreau."

"Gay Moreau!" Carson Drew exclaimed. "Chief, if that girl's responsible for Nancy's disappearance, my daughter is in great danger!"

CHAPTER XIX

No Escape!

EVEN as Carson Drew made the pronouncement that Nancy's life was in danger, his daughter was thinking the same thing. She was lying on the cabin floor where she had been thrown, and was trying to loosen the ropes which bound her.

Nancy glanced around the tiny cabin. It had two bunks, a table, and a chair. "Even if I could work myself free, there's no escape route," she thought.

The imprisoned girl looked toward the one tiny porthole. At this moment the cruiser began to roll heavily. The river must be getting rough.

Just then the cabin door was opened and Nancy felt a strong gust of wind. Jean Holmes entered the room and slammed the door shut. She gave Nancy a gloating look.

"Comfortable? Oh, I forgot. Our clever sleuth can't talk." The ex-waitress walked over and tore the cloth from Nancy's mouth. The girl's lips felt parched and dry.

Jean laughed mockingly. "I suppose you'd like a drink of water. Well, Carson Drew's daughter can stay thirsty. Thanks to him," she said bitterly, "I gave up most of the luxuries of life for quite a while!"

"Dad!" Nancy cried out. "What did he have to do with—" She broke off, suddenly recalling the waitress's startled reaction when Nancy's father had peered into the inn dining room. Nancy also remembered the Merriweathers' story.

"I think I understand," Nancy said. "It was my father who proved you were guilty of check forgery, Gay Moreau!"

The other girl seemed thunderstruck. But she quickly recovered her poise. "So you found out who I am. Well, it won't do you any good."

Gay's tone was sinister. Nancy remained outwardly calm; at least, she could stall for time.

"You're the girl who impersonated me in Burk's Department Store," the young detective accused. "Also, you played the parts of Jean Holmes and Mary Mason at Lilac Inn."

"You can call me Gay now," the girl sneered. "I had you fooled, though, didn't I? But then, I was a good actress before I went to jail. Your father represented one of the persons whose checks I forged. I told him the day I was convicted I'd get revenge."

Nancy nodded. "And you got your chance to do it by posing as Carson Drew's daughter," she said. "First you broke into our home and stole my charge plate, and the silver-framed picture to copy my appearance. You took a flowered dress of mine, too."

"That's right." Gay tossed her head defiantly. "The mink stole, evening gowns, and watch will fit into my new social life."

"And I suppose Emily's diamonds will, too?" Nancy prodded.

Gay smiled triumphantly. "Yes, I have the real jewels, and Emily Willoughby has the fake ones. A tidy haul. They're here in this cabin. We'll sell them for a fancy price where we've disposed of a few other things."

Gay began boasting of how the jewel theft had been accomplished. She said that after leaving jail she had not been able to find theatrical parts. Finally, she had forged references, and worked as Mary Mason for Mrs. Stonewell.

"After that," Gay went on, "my brother-in-law Bud, Gil Gary, Frank, and their pals came up with a sharp idea of buying the sub to use on the Angus River so no one could spot the place we were using as a hide-out. And that was why Gil and I went to work at Lilac Inn. Never mind that part now. Anyhow, while I was there I overheard Mrs. Willoughby tell that woman Maud when she was going to present the diamonds. I decided to steal them at the party. Gil turned off the lights at the right moment."

When Gil had phoned her that Nancy was at Lilac Inn, Gay said she had schemed her next move.

"To throw people off the track, I disguised myself as Jean Holmes and went to the Empire Employment Agency to ask for waitress work at Lilac Inn. What a break when I met Maud Potter there and got the job without registering at the agency."

"So that's why you came to the inn earlier for an interview," Nancy interjected. "Later you sneaked back, and hid in the secret closet."

"Yes. What made you guess *I* was the thief?"

Nancy explained about the lilac petals and other clues, including the note she had found which led her to Lillie Merriweather.

"Lillie!" Gay said scornfully. "Did she tell you that she was one of the people whose checks I forged?"

"No!" Nancy replied in amazement.

Gay sneered. "Lillie changed her mind and didn't prosecute—always felt sorry for me and her dad did too. I liked him. In fact, I stole Mr. Daly's blue pipe and mailed it to Mr. Merriweather. But Lillie's had all the stage breaks! I hated her, but never let on!"

Nancy stared at Gay unbelievingly. The former actress certainly had a twisted outlook on life!

Now Gay said she had put the note to Lillie in

an old apple tree for Frank to pick up and deliver. "But he didn't come—that John McBride was always snooping around. He even found our shack, but not what was in it. I finally managed to sneak the note away when the policeman turned his back."

"You decided," said Nancy, "to throw suspicion away from yourself by implicating Maud Potter."

"Sure," Gay admitted. "Maud Potter was a natural for your suspicions. So I figured you might believe she was the one who put the diamond in your purse. *I* did that, and got a friend of mine to bump into you at a good moment.

"Also, I was the mysterious girl Helen saw in the grove. Gil was the one who knocked Miss Corning out. He got panicky when he saw her, and thought she might not be fooled by the 'haunt' idea."

"And of course," Nancy said dryly, "you and I met face to face in the grove."

"*You* were the ghostly figure who jumped out at me?" Gay said, surprised. Then she laughed. "Pretty good impersonator yourself." She explained that on the night Nancy had encountered her, she had been in a hurry and forgotten to wear the dark wig.

Nancy's bonds were biting into her skin painfully. But she gave no sign of this as she asked Gay, "Did you print on a paper a message about pruning 'blue pipes'?"

"Yes. Bud told me to put it there for Gil. It meant the sub would arrive that night." Gay said that "blue pipes" had been used as a signal in other ways. The flowers she, as Jean, had placed in the dining-room window meant "Watch out for sleuths." Gay admitted also that the gang had tapped the inn's telephone wires after "Mary Mason" had left.

At that moment the cabin door opened. A man Nancy had not yet seen stood there. He was tall and dark, with thin features.

Gay introduced him as Simon, her fiancé. "You talk too much, Gay," he growled.

Ignoring Nancy, he added, "It's very foggy and the water's getting rougher. Frank and Gil are watching for patrol boats. Bud's steering."

Simon left. Gay then opened a large make-up kit. She took out two wigs. "Watch this," she told Nancy proudly.

The actress pulled off the brown wig she was wearing and put on a reddish-blond hairpiece. Then she applied long eyelashes and heavy rouge and lipstick.

"Meet Mary!" she said.

Nancy did not comment. Instead, she asked, "Did one of your pals throw a rock at my car?"

"Yes, as a warning, but you ignored it," Gay replied. "I knew through Gil you were suspicious. We were ready in case you hit Dockville."

Gay removed her Mary Mason make-up. "And

now, meet your double, Nancy Drew!" she said dramatically.

The captive sleuth watched as Gay deftly arranged her hair like Nancy's. Then, with eyebrow pencil and other cosmetics, transformed her face. Nancy had to admit the resemblance was striking.

"Incidentally," said Gay, "thanks for the loan of your pink dress. Wish I could have kept the date with that handsome John McBride."

"Tell me, who was responsible for the message phoned to Anna?" Nancy asked.

"Bud. He's a good mimic," Gay bragged. "And our skin diver threw the spear at you when Frank signaled."

"Whose idea was it to place the time bomb?"

"Mine," Gay replied. "But Gil put it in the cottage."

Gay now admitted that Bud's midget submarine was the object which had capsized the girls' canoe. He and Simon had been in the craft and were practicing a partial ascent as the girls passed over it.

"That was really just an accident," Gay added.

Nancy's mind dwelled on the submarine. Was it also part of Bud's "sharp idea"? She could get no answer from Gay about this.

The actress did admit that the gang was responsible for breaking in and turning on the phonograph record, stealing the lilac tree, and digging the hole into which Hank had fallen. They had also caused the inn to quake by using a strong vibrating machine against the cellar wall, then running off with it before being detected.

All these things had been done, Gay said, to make Emily and Dick close the inn and keep Nancy and the others from detecting the gang's project until they were finished in this locale and could make a getaway to another spot. "We knew you were finding out too much," Gay told Nancy. "So we had to act fast. The trouble was, nothing made you get out!"

On a sudden hunch, Nancy queried, "Does this other project of yours have to do with the missing tools?"

Gay hesitated. "That's something you'll have to figure out."

Just then, the boat dipped sharply. Gay clutched her stomach. "Oh, I feel terrible!" she cried, her face a grayish green. "I think I'm seasick!"

The impersonator slumped into a bunk. Nancy's eyes darted around the cabin, trying to guess where the diamonds might be. Certainly not in any of the obvious places. Her glance lingered on a wall barometer. This would be an ideal spot if its back were hollow!

Then the cabin door opened and Gil entered. "What's the matter with you, Gay?" he said roughly. "C'mon. We're headin' for shore till this blows over and the fog lifts."

"Oh, leave me alone!" Gay said irritably. "I'm ill."

The next moment there was a crash and the sound of splintering wood. Nancy was hurled headlong across the cabin, and Gil and Gay were flung to the floor. They heard cries from outside and someone shouting, "About, Bud! *About!*"

Gil was the first to recover from the crash. He dashed out of the cabin. In a minute he was back with Simon.

"We struck a log!" Simon gasped. "We're sinking! And there's a fire in the engine!"

"Besides, some boat's approaching!" Gil added. "Might be a patrol. Frank and the others have jumped over. We're scramming too, in the sub."

"Get up, Gay!" Simon ordered.

But the former actress, chalk-white, seemed unable to move. Simon rushed over and yanked the actress to her feet.

"The diamonds!" Gay screeched. "We can't forget them!"

"We can't be caught with loot," Simon argued. "We'll skin-dive for the diamonds later." He glanced toward Nancy. "I'd better cut her loose."

The man groped in his pocket for a knife, but Gay stopped him. "Don't be a fool!" she hissed. "If she drowns, we can't be blamed. Good-by, Nancy Drew!"

The trio raced from the cabin. Nancy, bound and helpless, was left alone in the sinking ship.

CHAPTER XX

Nancy's Citation

UNTIL now, Nancy had not fully believed that her captors would let her perish. But she was left, bound hand and foot, aboard a sinking vessel!

Suddenly Nancy sniffed the acrid smell of smoke —the fire was spreading! She screamed for help until her throat was hoarse. Then, about to faint, Nancy heard an answering shout, and the sound of a boat pulling up outside the porthole.

"Oh, thank goodness," she breathed fervently.

Shortly, two men in River Police Patrol uniforms hurried into the cabin. They quickly untied Nancy and carried her on deck. She saw that the fog had thinned and that the cruiser's stern was aflame. Desperately she tried to tell the men of the escaped gang, and what had happened.

"No time to talk now!" one of them urged.

The patrol boat stood near the bow of the cruiser, which was almost submerged. Nancy and the men quickly transferred to the other boat.

As the patrol craft pulled away, giant searchlights played over the surrounding waters. Captain Morgan, head of the patrol, came up beside Nancy in time to see the burning cruiser go under. Emily Willoughby's precious diamonds would soon be on the river bottom.

Nancy identified herself, and quickly explained about being taken prisoner and left in the sinking ship to drown. "You must capture the five men and Gay Moreau! Some of them are probably swimming to shore. The others went in the sub."

To her astonishment, the captain asked Nancy to look through a nearby porthole into a cabin where three men sat. "Recognize them?" he asked.

"Yes!" Nancy gasped. "Bud Mason, Frank, and the skin diver!"

Captain Morgan nodded. "We fished them out of the water just before rescuing you. They said they had jumped overboard after colliding with a fallen log—but nothing about any prisoner on the cruiser."

"Naturally!" said Nancy. "Hurry! You might still spot the sub if it hasn't submerged."

Captain Morgan looked dubious. Nevertheless, he barked an order. A high-beam searchlight was played over the water.

A moment later Nancy cried out, "Look!"

A shark-shaped object could be seen floating above water in the distance. Captain Morgan picked up binoculars.

"You're right, Miss Drew. It is a small sub!" he exclaimed. "Full speed ahead!"

Nancy waited tensely as the patrol craft pulled alongside the submarine. Gay, Gil, and Simon were inside it, with the hatch open.

Captain Morgan and his men gave the actress a startled look, then glanced at Nancy. The girl's heart sank. No wonder the men were confused! Gay still wore her Nancy Drew disguise!

"Gay Moreau has been impersonating me," explained Nancy, as the trio were helped aboard and towlines attached to the submarine. "She and the others are diamond thieves."

"This girl has been impersonating *me* for some time!" Gay snapped. "*My* name is Nancy Drew!"

The young sleuth started to protest, when Gay withdrew a wallet from the pocket of her dress. Nancy was dumfounded when Gay took out a driver's liccnse and handed it to the captain.

"This license was issued to Miss Nancy Drew of River Heights," the captain said, frowning.

Nancy realized that Gil must have stolen the license when he planted the bomb in the cottage! Gay smiled triumphantly. "*This* girl is the thief! She was tied up because she sneaked aboard our boat and tried to steal jewelry from my luggage."

Nancy realized that the actress in desperation had cleverly reversed the situation to keep from being arrested. No one aboard could, or would, identify the real Nancy Drew. If the gang's stories were believed the six might be released. Nancy could be taken into custody.

"By the time my identification can be established, the others will have recovered the diamonds and escaped," she thought desperately.

Just then, a foghorn sounded and the group on board saw a searchlight sweeping across the water. Moments later, a second patrol launch came into view and pulled alongside.

Gay Moreau had pushed forward to stand in front of the young sleuth. At the same time, Nancy and she recognized Carson Drew standing at the railing beside John McBride and Lieutenant Brice. Also present was Chief McGinnis.

"Nancy!" Mr. Drew called. "Oh, Nancy, my dear, you're safe!"

Gay smiled and waved back. Then she edged furtively toward the stern, as if intending to jump overboard.

Nancy, meanwhile, had been expecting such a move. Unnoticed by Gay she had backed up several feet. The next moment, as the actress hurled herself toward the rail, Nancy tripped her. Gay went sprawling on the deck.

"That's one score evened," Nancy said firmly.

But Gay was still undaunted as Carson Drew walked across a plank and was about to step onto the deck of the other craft. She leaped to her feet. Shoving Nancy aside, she dashed toward Mr. Drew.

"Dad—I'm so glad to see you!" she cried, and was about to fling herself into his arms when Nancy intervened.

"No, Dad, it's a disguise!" she exclaimed, and grasped Gay by the arm. With her free hand, she rubbed off some of the actress's heavy make-up.

As Gay stood glaring balefully, her true looks were disclosed. Carson Drew said severely, "Well, Gay Moreau, justice is catching up with you again." Then he kissed his daughter.

All this time Simon had been pinned against the railing by several of the police. Now he made a desperate effort to jump overboard, but was instantly stopped. "Well, I guess we've had it, Gay," he said grimly.

Gay's features were contorted with rage. "Next time we'll set a better bomb for you, Nancy Drew!" she screamed.

"There'll be no next time!" Chief McGinnis spoke sternly, as the river police officers put handcuffs on Gay, Gil, and Simon.

Brief explanations were made to Captain Morgan, who led the chief and Lieutenant Brice to the cabin where the other three captives were being guarded. The officials spent some time interrogating them while Nancy talked to her father and John McBride, bringing them up to date on the recent happenings.

"Gay almost had me fooled, until we came on board," Carson Drew admitted.

Later, in the captain's quarters, the officials met with Carson Drew, Nancy, and John.

"Nancy, you deserve an explanation from me," said John. "I told you once that my Army work was confidential. Actually I've been working on a case while visiting at Lilac Inn."

John stated that he was in reality a major at an Army missile base. "Some top-secret electronics parts had been stolen from the base, and suspicion fell on Frank Logan, a sergeant in the Engineers' Corps, who had been dishonorably discharged not long before the theft. Nothing was ever proved, but my mission was to follow up on the man and determine his guilt or innocence beyond a doubt."

The major had obtained a clue that Frank was in the River Heights area and finally traced him to the vicinity of Benton. John decided that staying at Lilac Inn, owned by his friend Dick, would be a good cover-up.

"One day, near the river, I came upon a piece of an engineer's insigne from the same branch Frank was in. This gave me an idea that he was in the vicinity. When you and Helen mentioned the man with the crew cut," John explained, "and his not trying to rescue you, I thought he might be Frank. Yet I had no luck pinpointing his whereabouts. That is, until I heard certain tools useful to an engineer and Dick's jig saw were missing. And when you found the metal device in the lilac grove, Nancy, I recognized it as a stolen electronics part. That reaffirmed my suspicions that Frank was nearby."

Major McBride continued, "I also learned that electronics parts were being stolen from shops and factories in this region, and the thieves were using a different stolen car or truck each time for their getaway, then abandoning it."

He told Nancy that the red panel truck was one of the vehicles used and Chief McGinnis explained to Nancy about finding it in Dockville, along with books on navigation and skin diving.

Nancy learned that Gay had discovered the river shack's old cellar when visiting the inn as a child. While working for Mrs. Stonewell, Gay had told Bud and his pals about the place and they hatched the scheme for storing the stolen parts there.

Some of the electronics equipment, John disclosed, was being sold on the black market at a town a hundred miles down the Muskoka River. By stealing the diamonds, Gay and the crooks would have enough money to live lavishly for a while until ready to start their nefarious scheme again.

"Were they the ones who used my convertible and left it in the lane?" Nancy asked.

John replied Yes, but only to cause one more annoyance. The major now explained that he had received permission from his superiors to talk with the police. "A black-market operator who was arrested tipped us off that the crooks from whom he was buying parts might be in Benton last night to arrange for a final getaway."

John said he had returned to Lilac Inn that evening in time to meet Mr. Drew, Chief McGinnis, who had come along during his free hours because of his interest in Nancy, and Lieutenant Brice. The trooper had just received word over the police radio of the accident to the cruiser. This, together with the fact that Carl Bard had seen Nancy go toward the river, had given John the idea that the men should board a patrol boat and search the sinking cruiser.

"This certainly has been an involved and dangerous mystery," said Carson Drew.

"Yes, and Nancy deserves most of the credit for solving it," the State Police lieutenant spoke up.

Nancy chuckled. "Don't forget, we still have to find Emily's diamonds. John, how about a skin-diving search by daylight tomorrow?"

"With pleasure." John grinned.

Everyone at Lilac Inn was relieved and thankful to learn that Nancy was safe and that the mysteries had been cleared up. The following morning the Willoughbys, Dick, and Helen came along to witness the treasure-diving expedition.

A river patrol launch stood by as Nancy and John skin-dived to the bottom of the Muskoka River. After locating the sunken cruiser, the couple boarded it and entered the cabin where Nancy had been imprisoned. The sleuth went immediately to the wall and took down the barometer. To her disappointment, the diamonds were not secreted there.

John and Nancy looked in every conceivable hiding place, but found no clue. Nancy racked her brains, trying to imagine what spot Gay would have chosen. A sudden hunch came to her as she spotted the actress's make-up case.

Nancy opened it, and searched among the contents. She picked out two tubes of lipstick. Nancy removed the tops and gasped.

The tubes were choked with glittering diamonds!

John gave Nancy a congratulatory pat on her shoulder. The girl detective put the lipsticks into a pouch attached to her waist and the divers surfaced.

Emily was thrilled upon recovering her jewels and tears came to her eyes. Dick and Mrs. Willoughby could not praise Nancy enough.

John beamed at his skin-diving companion. "One of your best deductions, Nancy."

A little later that day John announced that a salvage crew had raised the cruiser. A stock of valuable electronics parts was found in the small hold, including those Frank Logan had stolen from the missile base. The gang had planned to sell many of them to an enemy agent.

A week later Nancy was honored at a colorful

Army ceremony where she was presented with the Distinguished Civilian Service Medal for outstanding work.

"This is marvelous. Thank you!" she said.

When the young detective returned to Lilac Inn for a party on the eve of Emily's wedding, the bride-to-be gave her two attendants pins set with tiny diamonds. Nancy's was in the form of a lilac spray.

"I had this made especially so you'll never forget the mystery at Lilac Inn, Nancy." Emily smiled. "Dick and I will be forever grateful to you."

"So exquisite!" Nancy cried, and thanked her friend. "This was such a challenging mystery."

Secretly she wondered when another sleuthing adventure would come her way. "Soon, I hope," Nancy thought. She was to have her wish when she found herself involved in *The Secret of Shadow Ranch*.

Later, as Nancy, Helen, and Emily were talking, the two older girls suddenly stopped speaking on the subject of their forthcoming weddings. Helen said, "Goodness, Nancy, you must be tired of hearing us talk about steady partners when—"

Nancy interrupted. Laughing gaily, she said, "Not at all. For the present, *my* steady partner is going to be mystery!"

DETACH ALONG DOTTED LINE AND MAIL IN ENVELOPE WITH PAYMENT

Order Form
Own the original 56 thrilling
NANCY DREW MYSTERY STORIES®

In *hardcover* at your local bookseller OR
simply mail in this handy order coupon and start your collection today!

Please send me the following Nancy Drew titles I've checked below.
All Books Priced @ $5.99

AVOID DELAYS   Please Print Order Form Clearly

☐ 1	Secret of the Old Clock	448-09501-7	☐ 30	Clue of the Velvet Mask	448-09530-0
☐ 2	Hidden Staircase	448-09502-5	☐ 31	Ringmaster's Secret	448-09531-9
☐ 3	Bungalow Mystery	448-09503-3	☐ 32	Scarlet Slipper Mystery	448-09532-7
☐ 4	Mystery at Lilac Inn	448-09504-1	☐ 33	Witch Tree Symbol	448-09533-5
☐ 5	Secret of Shadow Ranch	448-09505-X	☐ 34	Hidden Window Mystery	448-09534-3
☐ 6	Secret of Red Gate Farm	448-09506-8	☐ 35	Haunted Showboat	448-09535-1
☐ 7	Clue in the Diary	448-09507-6	☐ 36	Secret of the Golden Pavilion	448-09536-X
☐ 8	Nancy's Mysterious Letter	448-09508-4	☐ 37	Clue in the Old Stagecoach	448-09537-8
☐ 9	The Sign of the Twisted Candles	448-09509-2	☐ 38	Mystery of the Fire Dragon	448-09538-6
☐ 10	Password to Larkspur Lane	448-09510-6	☐ 39	Clue of the Dancing Puppet	448-09539-4
☐ 11	Clue of the Broken Locket	448-09511-4	☐ 40	Moonstone Castle Mystery	448-09540-8
☐ 12	The Message in the Hollow Oak	448-09512-2	☐ 41	Clue of the Whistling Bagpipes	448-09541-6
☐ 13	Mystery of the Ivory Charm	448-09513-0	☐ 42	Phantom of Pine Hill	448-09542-4
☐ 14	The Whispering Statue	448-09514-9	☐ 43	Mystery of the 99 Steps	448-09543-2
☐ 15	Haunted Bridge	448-09515-7	☐ 44	Clue in the Crossword Cipher	448-09544-0
☐ 16	Clue of the Tapping Heels	448-09516-5	☐ 45	Spider Sapphire Mystery	448-09545-9
☐ 17	Mystery of the Brass-Bound Trunk	448-09517-3	☐ 46	The Invisible Intruder	448-09546-7
☐ 18	Mystery at Moss-Covered Mansion	448-09518-1	☐ 47	The Mysterious Mannequin	448-09547-5
☐ 19	Quest of the Missing Map	448-09519-X	☐ 48	The Crooked Banister	448-09548-3
☐ 20	Clue in the Jewel Box	448-09520-3	☐ 49	The Secret of Mirror Bay	448-09549-1
☐ 21	The Secret in the Old Attic	448-09521-1	☐ 50	The Double Jinx Mystery	448-09550-5
☐ 22	Clue in the Crumbling Wall	448-09522-X	☐ 51	Mystery of the Glowing Eye	448-09551-3
☐ 23	Clue in the Tolling Bell	448-09523-8	☐ 52	The Secret of the Forgotten City	448-09552-1
☐ 24	Clue in the Old Album	448-09524-6	☐ 53	The Sky Phantom	448-09553-X
☐ 25	Ghost of Blackwood Hall	448-09525-4	☐ 54	The Strange Message	
☐ 26	Clue of the Leaning Chimney	448-09526-2		in the Parchment	448-09554-8
☐ 27	Secret of the Wooden Lady	448-09527-0	☐ 55	Mystery of Crocodile Island	448-09555-6
☐ 28	The Clue of the Black Keys	448-09528-9	☐ 56	The Thirteenth Pearl	448-09556-4
☐ 29	Mystery at the Ski Jump	448-09529-7			

VISIT PENGUIN PUTNAM BOOKS FOR YOUNG READERS ONLINE:
http://www.penguinputnam.com/yreaders/index.htm

DETACH ALONG DOTTED LINE AND MAIL IN ENVELOPE WITH PAYMENT